Saving Trestan

A tail of the wild, the brave, and the foolish.

Written By

Laura Peirano

Published by Franklin Publishers

Printed in the United States of America

For permissions, inquiries, or additional copies, contact:

Franklin Publishers

www.franklinpublishers.com

N
E
S
W
Kingdom of Merrik
Santa Dalo Rosa
Kingdom of Duchaine
Daroogian Forest

Doomlock's
Castle

Table of Contents

Chapter 1: *Two Masters* — 1

Chapter 2: *The Horse Thief* — 7

Chapter 3: *The Charlatan* — 10

Chapter 4: *A Strange Request* — 19

Chapter 5: *The Secret Counsel* — 24

Chapter 6: *The Pure of Heart* — 33

Chapter 7: *A Man in a Sack* — 39

Chapter 8: *A Cruel Master* — 50

Chapter 9: *The King's Banquet* — 61

Chapter 10: *Gregor's Bedside* — 73

Chapter 11: *Gregor's Tea* — 81

Chapter 12: *Talk of War* — 91

Chapter 13: *An Unwanted Guest* — 99

Chapter 14: *Into the Mountains* — 109

Chapter 15: *Rattigan's Dungeon* — 120

Chapter 16: *Waiting for help* — 130

Chapter 17: *Sword Dancing* — 143

Chapter 18: *Finding Karegan* 158

Chapter 19: *Summoned* 171

Chapter 20: *Hunting Doomlock* 179

CHAPTER 1

Two Masters

 am Trestan, and the story which I am going to relate to you, little one, is a fairy tale. Now I'm aware that most fairy tales begin with 'Once upon a time.' However, my favorite story begins with the phrase, In the beginning, and so that is also how my tale shall start.

In the beginning, there was one Good Master. Nothing existed which he did not create. He was so good, mighty, and powerful that he was said to be the Almighty and Divine Master of all things. This Divine Master founded seven great kingdoms, and over each kingdom, he placed a high king to safeguard it.

All was right with the world. The seven kingdoms were like a garden of contentment for the people who lived there. But their peace and contentment came to an abrupt end when the other master came along. He was not good, Divine, or powerful. He was, however, terribly clever. And since he hated the Good Master with all of his might, he sought to destroy all that the Good Master had done. This usurper overthrew the high kings and replaced them with covens.

This continued until there were only two kingdoms left. The names of these two kingdoms were Duchaine and Merrick. Duchaine lay just on the south side of the Lusatian mountains, while Merrick lay just on the north side of them. These two kingdoms were like beacons of light in an otherwise dark, dreary world beset by cruel overlords and plagued by the occult, where human sacrifice was the norm and no human life was held as sacred, not even that of the unborn children.

This cruel master tried desperately to overthrow the last two kingdoms, and a violent struggle between the Divine Master and the usurper ensued. This struggle did not take place on a battlefield, but rather, it unfolded within the lives of specific individuals who did not yet belong to the cruel master. Princess Anetta was one of these ordinary individuals.

When Anetta was fifteen, her parents sent her to the Royal Court of Merrick at the request of Lady Rachel of Din Rock, Queen Regent of Merrick. Lady Rachel was a pious woman who had no children of her own. Since Anetta's parents had a great deal of esteem for the saintly lady, they gladly accepted her offer to take Anetta under her wing. Nothing could prepare Anetta's parents for what would happen next, though. Slowly yet surely, Lord Doomlock's coven snuck its way into the Royal Court of Merrick.

Now Lord Dinithall, King Regent of Merrick, was a far cry from saintly. Since the man did not learn to chastise his lower faculties in his youth, his ambition and lust for flesh became monsters that consumed the man. In the end, all that was left of King Dinithall was the monster of vice and sin.

Shortly after King Dinithall procured an odd pentagram tattoo on the palm of his right hand, his wife, Lady Rachel of Din Rock, fell ill. The king of Merrick made a bold and unmistakable advance towards Anetta one night. That was a night that Anetta would never forget. When she flatly refused the King's offer, she was drug away to be tortured until she changed her mind.

Now, King Dinithall was told to deliver Anetta to Lord Doomlock so that he could perform a ritual on her, which would make him the most powerful wizard in the seven covens. But King Dinithall also wanted power, and since he was only king Regent of Merrick, his days on the throne were numbered. In order for him to complete his ritual on her, King Dinithall had to get Anetta to commit a grave sin.

However, Anetta's purity was equal to her stubborn resolve not to offend her Divine Master, so she spent the next year in King Dinithall's wine cellar being tortured by Victor and Larson. By all rights, she should have died there. But somehow, she managed to escape and make her way back home. When Anetta finally made it back to her father's palace, she was very near death. Right after Anetta received the last rights from Father Rickmore, Lord Gregor, the captain of the palace guards, stuck his head into her room.

"Would my lady like to come to the King's Arena today and watch her brother practice swordplay?" Asked Gregor. Anetta was delighted by the idea.

"I would love to go!" Exclaimed Anetta emphatically. "However, I cannot walk. I am far too weak."

"Very well," said Gregor. "I will have the maids carry you out, girly, just as soon as you eat a bite of porridge."

As he said this, the captain of the palace guard produced a bowl from behind his back. Anetta scowled at him, but since she knew full well that Gregor wouldn't give an inch, she gave in and ate a bite of food. Gregor was good for his word, and he had Anetta carried out to the King's Arena.

Gregor came back to Anetta's chambers every day after that. Every time he came back, the captain of the palace guards made her eat more porage before he allowed her to be taken to the King's Arena. Anetta hadn't eaten anything since her return home until Gregor visited her with his bowl of food. Everyone was amazed when Anetta started to regain her strength once more.

Just as soon as Anetta was able to hold a sword Gregor began instructing her in sword play. The Queen Most certainly did not approve of Anetta's newfound occupation. However, everybody knew that Gregor had saved Anetta's life when he taught her how to use a sword. And the queen tried to keep her displeasure to herself.

King Dinithall was a coward, and Anetta had spent two years at her father's palace before King Dinithall arrived in Duchaine for the King's Tournament. Of course, King Dinithall was Doomlock's puppet, and he actually missed two years in the King's Arena after Anetta came home because he didn't have the Gaul to face King Ruben after what he had done to his daughter.

King Dinithall feared Lord Doomlock even more than he feared Anetta's father, however. So, after two years of missing the Tournament he had finally come to bring Anetta back with him.

Since the old king of Merrick claimed that Anetta was his runaway concubine and he was threatening war if she did not return home with him, Princess Anetta had a big problem on her hands. After brainstorming for nearly an hour to find a solution, Anetta finally came up with an idea. It was a risky idea. Anetta's mother certainly wouldn't approve of her plan of dissolving King Dinithall's alleged contract with her, but almost anything was better than going back to Merrick with that pig. He can't claim me if he's dead, thought Anetta as she braided her hair. Her fingers trembled as she fixed her hair, for she was about to take a plunge into the abyss, and she had no certainty. All she had was hope.

However, one should never underestimate the power of hope. When it is placed squarely in the Divine Master, hope is a very powerful force, and it drove Anetta to do something unthinkable. Anetta pulled her heavy, dark gray winter cloak over her shoulders because that day was bitterly cold. After pulling a bag of gold from underneath her pillow, Anetta headed out the door. She quickly passed through the great marble halls of the palace, past graceful columns of stone, and out the doors. A coach was waiting for her in a large courtyard.

When Anetta finally made it to where her coach was waiting, it took her a few moments to catch her breath. As soon as she caught her breath and was able to speak once again, she said, "Let's go, Gretchen, and make haste, for I really wish to beat my brother to the cathedral this morning."

When Anetta said this, Grinchin laughed heartily. Anetta and her brother Karegan often had a playful competition to see who could get to the cathedral for daily Mass first. This little game amused the old coachman immensely. Anetta usually didn't put much effort into beating Karegan to the cathedral. However, today was different for Anetta's plans depended heavily upon her getting there first. Grinchin was an old man with Gray hair and brown eyes. He had a rapidly receding hairline, and he was twice as wide as he was tall. His laughter was positively contagious, and Anetta had once threatened to have Gregor tickle him every morning so that she would have something to smile about. But Grinchin warned that if the Captain of the Palace Guard was ever to attempt such a feat, he would suffer a swift end. Anetta was only joking, of course.

However, she got the sense that the old coachman was not. When they arrived at the cathedral, Anetta told Grinchin that he was not to wait for her to get out of Mass, but rather, he should simply go back to the palace without her.

"But my lady "protested Gretchen, "How on earth do you expect to get back home without me?"

"Oh, I will just steal my brother's horse," said Anetta in a matter-of-fact way, as though Grinchin already knew what her plans were. However, Grinchin most certainly did not. He scratched his balding head for a moment or so. Then he said with a frown, "Well, perhaps I

should also avoid being seen by your mother, seeing that you're up to mischief."

"Yes!" said Anetta emphatically. "Please don't let my mother see you." The very first thing that Anetta did when she entered the cathedral was go looking for the celebrant priest, whose name was Father Gabriel. He was just leaving the confessional when she found him. The old priest kindly but firmly reminded Anetta that he was not able to hear her confession on account of the Queen's decree.

"Oh no, Father," said Anetta. "I was only wondering if you would be willing to do the exposition of the Blessed Sacrament after Mass today." As she said that, she handed the old priest her bag of gold. "Here, Father, this is for your trouble." The celebrant priest gave Anetta such a hard stare that the palms of her hands began to sweat.

After a few moments of awkward silence, he asked, "Is this a bribe, child?"

"Yes," said Anetta with a devious grin. The old priest sighed deeply. But he knew better then to ask any more questions. For you see, ignorance sometimes is bliss. Father Gabriel wanted to be able to claim that Anetta told him nothing if things didn't go as she had planned. Father Gabriel had to get ready for Mass quickly if he didn't want to be late. Before He turned to go, however, he said, "I'm leaving the sacristy open for you, child, so that you have a place to change your clothes."

After saying this, the good priest turned suddenly and disappeared through a doorway. Anetta was left wondering who Father Gabriel had been talking to, for he seemed to know exactly what she was up to without ever being told.

CHAPTER 2

The Horse Thief

hen the High Prince Karegan finally made it to the great cathedral, Anetta was already there in the pews waiting for Mass to start. On his way into the cathedral, Karegan bumped into Lady Ella. The two were dear friends, and Ella's half-brother Lackmore was like a brother to Karegan. The two young men spent much of their youth together. When Karegan's older brother died, it left a void in the life of the High Prince, which could only be filled with a brother.

Lackmore was probably grappling with his own loss as well after the death of his father. Lackmore seemed to seek out Karegan's company as a source of consolation in his grief. Karegan deliberately tried to ignore the bruise on Ella's cheek as he spoke with her. He knew full well that it was all the doing of her awful stepmother, Camilla, who was quite literally a witch.

"I am glad that you have finally decided to wash away all your ashes and soot this morning. You have been gifted with such a beautiful face, and it's a terrible shame to keep it hidden under all those ashes and soot." As Karegan spoke, he gave his friend a shy little smile of encouragement.

Ella did a great deal of penance for her brother Lackmore, who had taken it dark and dangerous path in life, and Karegan knew it. This is probably why she often had ashes and soot smeared on her face. Ella was also terribly embarrassed by the bruises as well. In fact, she would do almost anything to hide them from others. This meant that she would often go to Mass with her face smudged with ashes and soot. Of course, Ella could have just left home and entered a convent. But she made a vow to live with her stepmother until Lackmore had a conversion.

Karegan pulled a small parcel from under his cloak and handed it to Ella. His small package contained a little loaf of bread and two small cakes of cheese. The High Prince did this because Ella's stepmother Camilla rarely fed the girl, and Karegan was concerned for her well-being.

"Please come to my father's banquet tonight," begged Karegan as he handed Ella his little gift.

"I do not wish to sit next to your sister, Jezebel. I can't promise anything. However, I will do my best, seeing that it means so much to you," said Ella.

Just as Ella said this, her stepmother came around the corner, and the High Prince Karegan made himself scarce. As he turned and disappeared into the great cathedral, his two bodyguards, Dimitri and Malkovich, followed close behind him.

The first thing that Karegan noticed when he set foot in the cathedral was his sister Anetta sitting on a pew in the back and gloating over her victory. "Rats!" Murmured the High Prince as he took his usual place amongst the pews. He knew that Anetta was probably planning on rubbing his nose in his defeat. But little did he know that his sister was planning on doing something far worse.

Prince Karegan had once been led to believe that he could take holy orders like Brother John, who was also the youngest son of a king.

But he had a rude awakening when his brother Ruben died, and he was named High Prince and successor to the throne of Duchaine.

Karegan cried himself to sleep for months when he was sent away from his beloved Santa de La Rosa, and when the monks made him take off his habit, Karegan felt as though he was being skinned alive. Brother Raul predicted that he would forget his divine master just as quickly as the weather changed.

The man was dead wrong, though. Kerrigan went about like a young man in love with a beautiful woman, and he nearly swooned at the mere mention of his beloved. So it was no surprise to anyone when Karegan found himself lost in contemplation in front of the Blessed Sacrament.

When Malkovich discovered what Anetta had done, he hastened to inform the High Prince of what had taken place. But since Karegan was lost in contemplation, the man had to grab him by the shoulders and shake him vigorously to bring him back to earth. The High Prince left immediately for his father's palace on Dimitri's horse. Karegan rode his bodyguard's horse at breakneck speed. He felt sick as he rode, for he knew full well that his sister was probably up to no good, and he doubted that he would show up in time to stop her.

CHAPTER 3

The Charlatan

hen Mass was close to being over Anetta left the cathedral and went in search of her brother's horse. It didn't take long for her to find what she was looking for, either. Tied to Karegan's saddled was a sack that contained a lightweight sort of armor. Anetta took her brother's armor to the sacristy.

Father Gabriel had kept his word and left it open so that she had a private place to change. Anetta quickly changed into her brother's armor. Karegan had taken his armor with him that day so he could arrive at the King's Arena fully dressed and on time for his match with King Dinithall.

To Anetta's great delight, the armor fit her like a glove. In fact, the armor seemed to be made for her. This was probably because Karegan and Anetta were physically so much alike that the princess was almost a feminine copy of her twin brother. Of course, there were a few differences.

For example, Anetta had dark auburn hair and a fair complexion. While Karegan, on the other hand, had black hair and an olive complexion. He was also an inch taller than his sister. But they both had large dark eyes, thick black eyelashes, and a fine bone structure, high cheekbones and they were both tall and slender.

"I hope you will forgive me, brother," said Anetta as she put on her brother's helmet. She then mounted his horse and took off in the direction of her father's palace. As Anetta rode the horse in the direction of her father's palace, she mentally went over every penalty for horse theft in the Seven Kingdoms, and she felt quite sick to her stomach as she did so.

She dismounted her steed after crossing the drawbridge of her father's palace and handed the reins to the first manservant she met on her way to the King's Arena. Anetta held her breath every time she walked past someone who knew her for fear of being discovered.

However, if anyone suspected that it was her in her brother's armor, they did not let on that they did. When she finally made it to the King's Arena and the match between her and King Dinithall was about to start, she was approached by Lord Gregor, captain of the palace Guards.

"Are your daggers sharp?" Asked Gregor. Anetta, who had her visor down to hide her identity, would not dare answer Gregor verbally because she knew it would give her away. So she simply gave him a little nod of the head in response to his question.

Now Gregor suspected that it was Anetta all along because the princess had developed a bit of a limp during the year that she had spent as a guest in King Dinithall's wine cellar. But when she refused to answer him verbally, Gregor knew beyond the shadow of a doubt that he was right.

Gregor leaned in close and whispered, "Go for his left juggler, vain child. He's blind in his left eye, and it will be an easy target. Oh, and keep your helmet on, girly. If anyone discovers that it's you in that armor, there will likely be a terrible uproar amongst the crowd." Gregor then turned and left.

Anetta wondered if anyone else knew about her little ruse. Just then, Garic rode his horse across the drawbridge, and right behind him rode Karegan. As the young Prince rode his bodyguard's horse, he kept his hood down in hopes of hiding his identity. Both men took their horses to the stables, after which they headed for the King's Arena.

When he arrived at the King's Arena Karegan hid himself in the back of the stadium and prayed that no one would recognize him. Garic, on the other hand, went in search of King Ruben. Despite his great resolve to find the king as quickly as possible, Garic found himself terribly distracted upon entering the stadium.

The source of Garic's distraction was a group of men placing bets on the match. The men were obviously from Merrick, and they placed their bets on King Dinithall. Garic just couldn't help but stop and place a wager on the High Prince Karegan.

Someone announced that the match between the King of Merrick and the High Prince Karegan was about to start. The King and Queen of Duchaine were beaming with pride when the match was announced. This was to be Karegan's first year in the King's Arena. But his parents had no idea that it was Anetta who was about to enter the Arena, not her brother. It was a long-standing tradition for the High Prince of Merrick and the High Prince of Duchaine to have a sort of friendly sparring match in the King's Arena.

This event kicked off the King's tournament every year. If, for some reason, one of the two men were unable to fight in the Arena, the king of that country would take his place.

Now, the High Prince of Merrick had been missing for quite a long time, and there was even a rumor suggesting that he was dead. This was only a rumor, though. In fact, the High Prince of Merrick was very much alive and living at the Santa De La Rosa until the time came for him to claim his birthright. Because Alexander the Third, High Prince of Merrick, was missing, King Dinithall took his place in the Arena.

The King's Arena was a large octagon-shaped piece of dirt. It was surrounded on all sides by a short wooden wall in order to protect the people in the surrounding stadium. Both Anetta and King Dinithall entered the Arena through two little gates on the opposite side of the short wall.

When the match was announced, the two opponents entered the Arena almost in unison. The smell of fresh food, which was being sold by vendors, hung in the air, and it made Anetta feel even more queasy than before. It was a cold day, yet she was far too focused on what she was about to do to notice the chilling north wind that had begun to blow.

The armor that King Dinithall wore was shiny silver, and it was inlaid with gold filigree. He wore an open helmet, and it was easy to see the scar that ran across the left side of his face. His armor was made for battle, not for sparring, so it was really quite heavy. King Dinithall was a short, fat man. He had a receding hairline, and his hair was long and Gray. He held his hair back in an intricate braid, and if it wasn't tucked in his armor it would have reached down to his waist.

The armor which Anetta wore, however was painted dark blue and inlaid with silver. Her armor was so dark, in fact, that it was almost black in appearance, and the silver embellishment on it made a beautiful contrast against its dark blue color. Anetta's armor was designed for the King's Arena and it was much lighter weight than that which her opponent wore.

Anetta's original intention for wanting to kill King Dinithall was self preservation. However, when she saw the old king's face for the first time as she stepped into the Arena, her motivation switched momentarily to vindication. King Dinithall's face haunted Anetta's nightmares and she still had a hard time sleeping without having a lamp lit for her. There were huge holes in her memories, and those memories came back to her in nightmares. She wasn't safe, even in her sleep. She carried a dagger on her person at all times because it made her feel safer. Anetta was furious because she felt like she had been robbed. She was robbed of her memory, robbed of her safety, robbed of her reputation, and robbed of her dignity. Anetta had been trained in the King's Arena, and she knew every inch of it like the back of her hand. She found herself counting down the steps to King Dinithall.

When she reached the place where the old King of Merrick stood, she sheathed her daggers. Hot tears of rage ran down her face, and they seemed to leave burn marks on her cheeks. She pivoted on one leg and kicked the Old King's square in the chest. The King of Merrick went sprawling across the arena when Anetta did this, and since he dropped his sword, he was an easy target. Anetta picked up her opponent's weapon and quickly made her way toward where King Dinithall lay on his back with the wind knocked out of him. The crowd cheered loudly for Anetta when she knocked King Dinithall on his back, but she didn't hear them because she was too caught up in the moment. In fact there were a lot of things that Anetta did not notice.

For example, King Dinithall was taunting the High Prince of Duchaine when he entered the Arena. There was also a small group of palace guards who had gathered in the stadium, and they were cheering for her louder than almost anyone else in the crowd. Among the palace guards were Lord Gregor, Michellie, and Arlo. Anetta would have ended King Dinithall's life quickly.

However, just before she could reach him, three other men entered the arena by leaping over the short wall. Two of the men were wearing black velvet. Their names were Victor and Larson, and they both had poisoned daggers on them. The third man looked much like a gypsy because his long black curly hair was tied back with a red silk sash. He had a long, bushy black beard and mustache. His cheeks were sunken, and his old, gray, woolen clothes were covered in patches. The name of this man was Garic. He had come to protect the High Prince Karegan from Victor and Larson. Since Anetta didn't know this, however, Garic was the first man to be deprived of his sword, kneed in the chest, and thrown out of the King's Arena. Victor and Larson were the next to go. But they got far rougher treatment than Garic did.

Now, maybe it was just because they gave her more resistance than Garic did, or perhaps she just remembered the year that she had spent in King Dinithall's wine cellar being tortured by the two thugs. Whatever the case was, Anetta made a point to mop the floor with Victor and Larson before she threw them out of the King's Arena. When she was once again alone with the King of Merrick, she picked his sword up off the ground with the intention of ending his life swiftly.

When Anetta got into her little scuffle with Victor and Larson, she lost her helmet, and her hair became terribly disheveled. In fact, only the top of her hair remained pulled back out of her face because she had made a point to tie it back with a ribbon when she braided it. When the people in the stadium realized that it was Anetta in the King's Arena, they cheered for her wildly. She didn't hear them, though.

In fact, she hardly even noticed that she had lost her helmet, so focused was she on killing the old King of Merrick. Anetta looked like an avenging Angel as she made her way toward where King Dinithall was still picking himself up. Perhaps he recognized the girl he had tortured for a year coming for him with a sword in her hands and murder in her eyes.

Whatever the case be, King Dinithall let out a squeal of terror. He tried desperately to escape by scurrying away on his hands and knees. Anetta stopped him, though, by placing a foot on his back and pressing down. King Dinithall was sure that his life was over at this point. Something completely unexpected happened, though. King Ruben of Duchaine stood up and entered the arena. When he stood up, the stadium went so quiet that one could almost hear a pin drop.

Anetta's father entered the arena through one of the little gates. He just stood there for a moment or so, staring at his daughter. Neither of them spoke a word to each other, but it was quite clear to everyone that Anetta's father was pleading for King Dinithall's life. This wordless conversation only lasted for a brief moment.

Then King Ruben left the arena once more and went back to his seat. After that Anetta helped King Dinithall up roughly, heaved him up over the short wall, and threw him into the stadium. She then made herself scarce.

When the King of Duchaine made it back to his seat, he remained standing long enough to announce that the match was a draw. Sure, women weren't really allowed in the King's Arena, but King Dinithall had also broken the rules as well by bringing his two bodyguards along with him.

When Anetta lost her helmet in the arena, she had given the whole kingdom of Duchaine something to talk about. And the women at her father's palace were the worst *gossips* that ever lived. Anetta was sharply reminded of this fact as she made her way back to her bed chambers.

"Oh, how clever our old King is," said the head cook to one of the younger maidservants. Watching two kings fighting it out in the arena was getting old and boring, but putting three bodyguards into the mix was exciting to watch. And when Lady Anetta was also thrown into the mix, things got even better. Anetta rolled her eyes when she heard them talking. She was only glad that everyone believed that this fight was rigged in an attempt to entertain the people in the stadium.

When Anetta finally made it back to her bed chamber, she changed into her own clothes, sunk her face in a pillow, and wept bitterly. Anetta had always feared that King Dinithall would come to bring her back to Merrick with him. Learning how to fight had once given her a great deal of hope.

A hope that she might be able to avoid such a fate. But that hope was now gone. It had vanished like a small cloud of smoke in a stiff breeze. The worst thing, though, was that she had let her parents down. In fact, she may have even started a war with Merrick.

While Anetta sat on her bed weeping, there was a knock at the door. She felt reluctant to answer it, however, because she knew full well that her mother would want to speak to her sooner or later. Her fears were set to rest when she heard Gregor's voice on the other side of the door. "You can open up, girly," said the captain of the palace guards. "It's only me."

Anetta got up and opened the door promptly. When the door was open, Gregor held out a Snow White handkerchief for the Princess Anetta. Now, there was a vicious rumor circulating which stated that Gregor and Anetta had a love interest for each other. But nothing could be further from the truth. Gregor was simply like a kind uncle to Anetta, and that was all.

While Anetta scrubbed at her tears with Gregor's white handkerchief, Karegan stuck his head out from behind the captain of the palace guards and said, "I want my armor back, sis."

Anetta did indeed give her brother's armor back. However, since she was feeling quite ornery, she gave it back slowly, one piece at a time. "Now that you're done being cute," said Karegan as he closed the bag full of armor. "Oh, mother wanted to speak to you. What should I tell her?"

"Tell her that I have contracted the Black Plague," said Anetta with a scowl.

"Oh, I'll just tell her that you aren't feeling well. Said Karegan with a little chuckle. After saying this, her brother turned and disappeared down the hall along with the captain of the palace guards.

Shortly after leaving Anetta's room, Karegan bumped into Dimitri and Malkovich. When this happened Karegan handed Gregor his sack full of armor and sent him to put it away for him. After getting rid of his armor, the High Prince headed in the direction of his father's secret council meeting. Karegan wasn't in the least bit angry with Anetta for what she had done. In fact, he was rather glad that she took his place in the arena. For you see, he probably would not have spared King Dinithall's life, not even if his father had begged on his hands and knees.

In short, the hand of Divine Providence could be clearly seen in the situation. Gregor found himself in high spirits as he walked the King's great palace halls in the direction of Karegan's bed chambers. And since he thought he was completely alone, he broke out in song. Little did he know that a witch assassin was lurking just around the corner, waiting to put a poison dagger into his rib cage.

CHAPTER 4

A Strange Request

netta sat on the foot of her bed with a brush in one hand and a handkerchief in the other one. As she sat there, she cried her eyes out. Anetta had grown up hearing stories about Brother John. It was said that he could speak and understand many different languages without ever studying them. He had also been known to bring the dead back from the grave on more than one occasion.

Of course, this was all the work of the Divine Master and not some sort of magic trick. An idea suddenly crept into Anetta's head as she sat there weeping on her pillow. Perhaps Brother John could help her. She leaped off the edge of the bed and left her room quickly. She made it halfway to where Brother John was staying when she suddenly realized that she was still holding the brush in her hand. She went back to her room, set the brushed down, and put on a hooded cloak to hide the fact that her hair needed brushing. She then set out once more with the resolution to see Brother John. When she came to a small door made of oak, she knocked on it.

"Who is it?" Asked a voice from the other side of the door. It was not Brother John who answered her, though. Anetta's blood began to boil when this happened. How dare they place guards to watch Brother John, thought Anetta. It was bad enough that he was being held against his will, but having soldiers watch the saintly old priest was a new kind of low, even for King Dinithall.

"I am the daughter of the King!" said Anetta in a thundering voice. "Open this door at once, or I'll have you…" Anetta didn't get to finish her threat, though, because the door was quickly opened. It was opened with so much force, in fact, that it almost knocked her over.

"What is wrong with you?" Asked Anetta angrily. A man stepped out of the room before she could say anything else. Anetta's face turned 7 shades of red when she suddenly realized that she was standing face-to-face with Brother John.

"Leave us," said the old monk in a commanding voice, and the two soldiers left promptly.

Anetta entered the room and brother Jon shut and latched the door behind her. "I've been waiting for you, child," said the old monk as he latched the door.

"What took you so long?"

"Oh, I was just sitting in my room sulking," said Anetta as she shrugged her shoulders.

A broad smile split Brother John's lips when she said this because, judging by her rough appearance, Anetta was probably telling the truth. She stood and observed the man in front of her for a moment or so. Brother John had tonsured golden hair and a short beard. His large blue eyes were kind.

The old priest was rather short, which Anetta found quite surprising given the fact that all of his other half-brothers were giants. In fact, Brother John only stood 5 foot 2 inches tall. It was believed, though, that since he was fond of austerity in his youth, his lack of food had stunted his growth.

Brother John pulled a stool out of a corner for Anetta to sit on. Then he turned around and sat down in front of a little writing desk and began jotting down a list. The list was of an assortment of things which he needed to perform his priestly functions. So said he in a quiet voice, "What brought you here today?"

"Well," said Anetta. King Dinithall wants to bring me back home with him. I've been told that you have more than once brought the dead back to life with your prayers. And I was wondering if you prayed over me, would I die? Mother says that I must either leave here with King Dinithall or with Lord Lockland so that a war can be prevented."

"Father, I would rather die than become a… An object of lust," said Brother John as he dropped his quill on his piece of parchment.

A pain shot through the old priest as his pin fell. Oftentimes, people came to him because they wanted to be cured of some sort of affliction. They were usually in pain, but they always wanted to live. So he found himself puzzled over this sad and unusual situation.

Anetta had her back to the old priest so she didn't see him getting up and going over to where she was sitting. Brother John gave Anetta a little shove, and she slid to the floor on her knees. Now, Brother John had intended to ask Anetta when she made her last confession, but he ended up doing what the other monks of the Santa Della Rosa called babbling.

Brother John was weeping profusely over Anetta, and since her hood fell off, she had nothing to keep Brother John's tears off her bare head.

"You're raining on me Father" complained Anetta because her hair started getting wet with John's tears.

"Here," said Anetta as she held out her handkerchief. "It's only wet with tears, Father, I promise."

The pious old priest reached out a hand and took the handkerchief. He then went back to his little writing desk. But this time, he knelt with his back towards Anetta. When he did so, he asked, "When did you make your last confession, child?"

"It's been a long, long time," admitted Anetta with a sigh. "Mother and I had a disagreement some time ago. To punish me for my stubbornness, she has forbidden every priest in Duchaine from giving me any of the sacraments unless, of course, I'm dying." Anetta thought that she heard John snickering when she gave him the handkerchief, but she wasn't sure. This time, however, she was certain that he was laughing at her.

"So you have sort of been excommunicated by your mother because she lost her temper with you?" said John. "Oh, your poor father! It's fortunate that nobody has ever taught your mother how to use a weapon. That would be disastrous!" Brother John was obviously trying his best to contain his amusement over the situation.

"Oh, Father, I can't ever imagine my mother being in need of a weapon. She's positively a force of nature." This little comment from Anetta left the little old Mystic in stitches.

"I'm expecting someone else child and I'm running out of time, so I'll just give you a general absolution." For her penance, she was to brush her hair, say two Ave's, kiss her mother, and tell her that she loved her.

Now, Anetta really did love her mother. But she hadn't kissed her on the cheek since she was really quite little. To make things even more awkward, Anetta and her mother weren't really on speaking terms. Anetta would have rather been given a hard fast for penance, and Brother John knew it. This is why he probably gave it to her as a penance and not a suggestion.

After speaking with Anetta for a bit, the pious old mystic consecrated a host and gave half of it to her. The other half he carefully folded up in a clean white handkerchief and set it on the desk. After this, he practically shoved her out the door and latched it behind her. Once Anetta had gone, Brother John quickly cleared off the desk, unfolded his handkerchief on the desk, and fell to his knees in adoration of his Divine Master.

To Brother John's great delight, Garic was terribly late in coming to see him. Anetta had offered to have Rockbridge and Thornfield strung up in the King's courtyard but Brother John insisted that Rockbridge and Thornfield were not sent to guard him. Rather, they were his companions and his dearest friends. This wasn't entirely true, though.

Since Brother John was captured, the man had escaped several times. Rockbridge and Thornfield were soldiers scheduled to be executed for the crime of treason. Larson thought it would be amusing to have them stay with Brother John. If Brother John escaped again, he would be forced to watch Larson torture the two soldiers to death. This was enough to keep the little, kind-hearted old monk in his place, at least for the time being.

CHAPTER 5

The Secret Counsel

ing Ruben left his bed chambers and headed towards the secret council meeting. He made his way threw a series of hidden passageways long forgotten by most of the palace servants.

The corridor through which he passed smelt damp. There was the sound of dripping water coming from somewhere in the distance. As he walked, the old king of Duchaine pondered what Brother John had told him in the stadium.

Brother John said that King Ruben's death was imminent and that Karegan would not sit long on his father's throne. John also said that the next King of Merrick would also someday rule Duchaine.

What did the little old Mystic mean by that? Was his beloved Duchaine to lose her sovereignty? These and many other questions bounced around King Ruben's head as he sauntered through the dimly lit passageway. The King of Duchaine was running just a little bit late.

This was because he had stopped in on his wife to make sure she was ok. The Queen had fainted when Anetta lost her helmet in the arena. And although she was fine, King Ruben was apt to worry about his wife. He found the door, which he was looking for quite easily. When he opened it, the first thing he saw was Garic and Gregor waiting for the council to start. While they waited, the two men carried on a lively conversation.

It had been quite some time since the two brothers had seen each other, for you see, they had a lot of catching up to do. When King Ruben entered the small room, the Captain of the Palace Guards approached him and whispered something in his ear. The King frowned for a moment, then nodded his head and consent. Gregor then left the room for a bit.

When he came back, he had a sack full of something which he left in the corner. The captain of the Palace Guards went back to talking with Garic as if nothing had happened.

Soon, Karegan entered the room. Just behind the High Prince came Dimitri and Malkovich. The first thing that Karegan did was greet his father by kissing him on the cheek.

"I'm sorry, I'm just a little bit late," said Karegan. "Lobos has been carrying things off again. This time, he took a sack of things that Lord Lackmore and I had put together for Brother John."

"A prince should never apologize for being late, my son," whispered the king as he returned his son's kiss.

After speaking with his father briefly, Karegan went to see Lord Garic. The old Deacon was far less cultured than the king was. And since Garic was feeling ornery he greeted the Prince by putting him in a headlock.

"How have you been… you old fart," gasped Karegan as his face turned red on account of him being choked by Garic. After a brief struggle, the young Prince reached up and punched Garic in the stomach. This knocked the wind out of the old Deacon, and he released his death grip on Karegan.

"Please never do that again," choked the High Prince as he straightened himself up. "You smell like a goat."

"I missed you too, your Majesty." Said Garic with a devious grin. "I heard a girl stole your horse this morning while you were daydreaming."

"OH, yeah," said Karegan. "I saw that very same girl give you a whooping in the King's arena this morning. I'd gladly be thrown out of the King's arena dozens of times if I could see your sister mop the floor with those two criminals again. That was epic!"

"I think I enjoyed it even more than you did," admitted Gregor with a devious grin.

As they were talking, Father Rickmore finally arrived. He was even more tarty than the High Prince was. This is probably because he was a very old man, and age had slowed him down to a snail's pace.

The little old priest walked with a hobbling gait because he had fallen and broken his hip at some point. Father Rickmore used to be a tall man but now he was shrunken and bent by age.

The old priest was so bent, in fact, that he resembled a question mark. What was left of his once dark hair was now white and shoulder length. He was cleanly shaven. The old priest was going blind because he had cataracts, and every time he spoke, he practically shouted because he was also going deaf as well.

Father Rickmore wasn't really a member of King Ruben's secret council, however the King of Duchaine refused to start his secret counsel without his confessor being present. This was on account of the great esteem he had for the pious old priest.

When Father Rickmore entered the room, Garic and Gregor huddled in the corner along with Karegan's two bodyguards in order to place bets on how old they thought Father Rickmoore was. Karegan soon joined the little huddle.

"This is what we'll do." Said the High Prince. "I will go figure out how old father is, and the two biggest losers will lick the floor."

Now, no one really cared how old Father Rickmore was. The little wager simply served as a childish amusement while they were waiting for the secret counsel to start. And it was taking longer than usual for Father Rickmore to take his seat. The King's confessor got halfway to his seat when he was accosted by Karegan.

The High Prince offered him his arm for support. When Karegan did this, the old priest looked up, gave the High Prince a toothless grin, and murmured something that sounded much like Children.

As they walked, the High Prince asked a series of questions. It most certainly would have been rude for him to ask Father Rickmore straight up how old he was. The High Prince was very clever, though. And he knew full well that old priests are very much like old married women. That is, they like to brag about how long they have been bound by the sacrament of their vocation. Father Rickmore was no exception either.

"How long have you been a priest, Father?" Asked Karegan.

"Well, let me see," said Father Rickmore. "That was right before your grandfather took the throne. It was 70 years ago. I was only 19 at the time, but I remember it vividly because it marked the beginning of a religious persecution."

"Wait," said Karegan. "I thought my grandfather stopped the persecution when he ended the Inquisition."

"He did. But once the Inquisition was ended, another persecution began. This was a religious persecution, and the mere mention of God was considered offensive. In those days, men of my profession lived in fear. Those who had the audacity to preach the gospel weren't safe from exile. It's no wonder that the Seven Covens gained so much power in that brief period of time."

Father Rickmore suddenly stopped talking when he realized that he was standing right in front of his chair.

After helping the old priest take his seat, Karegan went to get a chair of his own. Karegan deliberately bumped into Garic on his way to the pile of wooden chairs in the back of the room.

When he did so, he whispered, "Gregor and Malkovich lick the floor."

Gregor, who heard Karegan, groaned. But a man's word is a man's word, and after all, he did agree to the little wager.

Everyone sat in a sort of semicircle. On King Ruben's right sat his confessor, and on his left sat the High Prince Karegan. The King and his son not only resembled each other in appearance, but they also had the same attitude as well. Of course, there were some differences between them, though.

For example, the High Prince was quite a bit taller than his father. They also wore their hair differently. Karegan's hair was long and straight. He had it tied back with a hemp cord at the nape of his neck.

King Ruben, on the other hand, had both sides of his head shaved. His remaining hair was held back in an intricate braid which hung halfway down his back. He had a short beard and mustache, while his son had not yet been able to grow any facial hair at all. If Karegan kept tradition, however, his hair would stay at one length until the death of his father. The sides of his head would then be shaved, and his remaining hair would be held back in a braid.

On the other side of Karegan sat Dimitri and Malkovich. The two bodyguard's looked like blue-eyed hawks. Both men had short beards. They wore their hair long and it was held out of their face in intricate braids which hung halfway down their backs. They both had similar features, and given their age difference, they were most likely father and son, and they spoke with heavy foreign accents.

They were probably defectors from some foreign military because the two men had even more discipline than Brother John did. Dimitri was in his 50s, like Garic, and his blonde hair had started going white. One could hardly tell, though, because it blended so well with his hair color.

Malkovich, on the other hand, was still in his 30s, and his hair was still quite gold. They both were just half an inch shy of seven feet tall. They had broad shoulders and a muscular build. Both men were part of Garic's little band of horse thieves when he was living with Gregor as a Fugitive.

Garic sat on the other side of Father Rickmore. Next to him sat his brother Gregor. The two brothers had the same body type. They had broad shoulders and were sturdy built. They both stood a hair under 6 feet and they had large dark eyes. However, their resemblance stopped there. Garic had a mess of curly black hair and a mustache and beard that matched it. Gregor, on the other hand, only had one eyebrow, and he wore a blue silk sash over his bald head.

Once everyone was seated King Ruben gave the High Prince Karegan a little nod of the Head. When he did so, the young Prince stood up and addressed the secret council. He spoke in a clear, confident voice. The only indication that Karegan was nervous was the fact that he kept playing with the cuffs of his sleeves.

"My dear friends, this council was first started by my grandfather when all of his council members were either hung for treason or sent into exile for the same crime. War hangs over our heads like ominous storm clouds promising great destruction. King Dinithall claims that my sister is his concubine. He says that if we don't hand Anetta over to him, he will declare war on us because we are harboring a fugitive of Merrick."

"King Dinithall loves his comfort far too much. It isn't likely that he will declare war if we don't comply with his demands," said Father Rickmore with a scowl.

"That's true," admitted Karegan. "But King Dinithall is a puppet. I wouldn't be surprised if Doomlock sent Victor and Larson here just to make sure that the King of Merrick does what he's told to. In fact, King Dinithall is probably going to disappear once Doomlock is finished with him."

"But it's all a lie!" Shouted Gregor angrily as he stood up from his seat. "We all know that Anetta never gave in to that pig!"

"That doesn't mean that she wasn't forced to sign some sort of document, said Garic calmly. A person might do anything if you torture them enough."

When Gregor stood up, Garic remained seated in his chair. "Why on earth did you stop her from killing him in the King's arena? He couldn't claim her if he was dead!" Shouted Gregor angrily. This was most certainly not the proper way to speak to a king but the old king of Duchaine didn't seem to mind all that much.

"Keep your shirt on, brother." Said Garic in a calm voice. "Anger has never been known to solve a problem."

The King of Duchaine stood up when Gregor accused him of being foolish, and he calmly defended his decision to save the King of Merrick. When King Ruben stood up, everyone who was still seated stood as well out of respect for their king.

"Killing King Dinithall would not have prevented a war, and Brother John strongly advised against it anyway," said the old king. It was as if King Ruben was speaking to equals rather than subordinates.

"Did Brother John tell you how to break Anetta's contract with King Dinithall?" Asked Garic as he rubbed the palms of his hands together nervously.

"Yes, he did," said King Ruben.

"Well," said Garic and Karegan almost at the same time. Brother John suggested that Anetta get engaged to someone in order to break the alleged contract.

"But with whom?" Asked Garic eagerly. King Ruben raised a bushy eyebrow as he rubbed his chin thoughtfully, and a mischievous smile came to his lips.

"No!" said Garic. "You can hang me for treason if you like, but my answer is still no!"

The old Deacon and the king of Duchaine turned to face one another, and they had a brief sort of stair down.

After a moment or so of awkward silence, King Ruben said, "I don't want you to break your vow, Garic. I'm simply asking you to put on a ruse tonight for my daughter's sake. That is, I am going to announce your engagement to Anetta at my banquet tonight. I want you to just play along with me."

"What do you want me to do with her after the banquet tonight?"

"I want you to take Anetta into the mountains and lock her away in a convent where she'll be safe." Garic put his hands on his hips when King Ruben said this. Garic's posture made him look very much like a defiant teenager, while King Ruben looked much like Garic's stern father. This was despite the fact that they were only a few years apart in age.

This is because the old king was going Gray much quicker than Garic was. In fact, most of King Ruben's hair was now silver.

"Can't you just find a rich lord to marry her?" Retorted Garic as he crossed his arms over his chest.

"No. Her reputation has been completely ruined by that pig. Besides, Anetta has developed a strong distrust for men."

"Ok," Said Garic, as he let his arms fall to his sides. "Why don't you just have Gregor do it?"

"Because your brother is dying." Said the King in a soft voice as he struggled to hide his grief.

Garic's face went white when the king said this, and he looked as though he was about to faint as he stumbled backward into his chair.

Everyone else in the room remained stoic except for Karegan, who was obviously grief-stricken.

"I will do it!" said Garic in a hoarse voice, and everyone in the room knew that he was speaking to Gregor and not the king.

Gregor and Anetta first met when the former captain of the palace guards had been executed for the crime of treason. Some sort of mix-up was made, and Gregor was summoned to the palace by mistake.

Gregor was about to be sent away, but Princess Anetta, who was only three years old at the time, came barging into the room uninvited. She crawled into Gregor's lap, and no bribe or threat of punishment could move the child.

The old king saw this as a sign, and he made Gregor captain of his palace guards. This was despite the fact that Gregor's face was terribly disfigured by burn scars. Garic knew full well that Anetta was like a daughter to Gregor, and it was the only reason that the old Deacon gave in to King Ruben.

The Pure of Heart.

When King Ruben's secret council meeting came to an end, everyone knelt for a blessing from Father Rickmore. Afterward, everyone dispersed.

Garic went to see Brother John right away. Gregor was planning on joining Garic in John's room, however he first had to take care of something. Gregor was simply going to go take his sack to his own bed chambers where its contents would be safe.

However, Michellie informed him that his room was being watched by Victor and Larson. So Gregor just took it back to Garic's room instead and left it there. The thing which Gregor hid under his brother's bed was soon forgotten by the captain of the palace guards.

When Garic came to the room where Brother John was staying, the door swung wide open before he could even knock on it.

"Come in," said a voice from inside the room.

When Garic entered the room, he noticed Thornfield and Rockbridge right away. They were standing on either side of Brother

John and talking to him. Both men left the room promptly after Brother John gave them a hand gesture.

As soon as they were gone, Brother John embraced and kissed Garic on his forehead, much like a father might. And as John kissed him, he said, "It has been too long, my son. Where's your brother Gregor?"

"He will be along shortly," said Garic as he tried desperately to free himself from Brother John's death grip. The old Deacon couldn't breathe, and he felt like his ribs were about to crack.

Finally, when Garic did manage to free himself, he asked, "How's everyone at the Santa de La Rosa?"

"Brother Lucas is dead," said John as he stroked his beard in an effort to remain calm. "He rebuked Victor sternly when he came to take me away from the Santa Dalo Rosa. Brother Lucas was stabbed in the chest because he came to my defense."

"No!" Said Garic. "He's one of the main reasons that Gregor and I grew into the men we are today. We owe so much to him."

"I also owe a great deal to that saintly old Monk," admitted Brother John as he fought back tears. "It was Brother Lucas who had first introduced Father Ivan and me to chanting the Divine Office. Lucas was a great father figure to me in my youth, and he played a large role in my spiritual development."

"Gregor's seizures have returned," said Garic. "You know what Father Ivan predicted?"

"Yes," said Brother John gravely. "I always hoped he was mistaken. However, I have never known him to be wrong about such things. That was the first time I met you and Gregor. Although that was a long time ago, I remember it quite well. That was when Father Ivan and I were still living as hermits in the great mountains. It was the middle of winter. You came to the door of my cell in the dead of night, and you were carrying your brother in your arms. He was so badly burnt I was sure he was going to die. Just when all seemed lost, Father Ivan came rushing into my hermitage. He was holding a piece of parchment in his hand. On the parchment was scribbled an act of consecration to the Blessed Virgin. It promised never to look at a girl with romance in one's heart or marriage on one's mind. The funny thing, though, is that it also renounced every crime ever committed by a boy and rhymed perfectly."

"I bet Father Ivan was a terror in his youth," said Garic as he choked back laughter. His mirth was shortly lived, however, because Brother John reminded him that this was the night on which Father Ivan had made his prediction. Ivan said that when Gregor's seizures returned, he would die. Garic suddenly stopped talking, and he looked around the room.

"Where have you hidden him?" Asked Garic in a quiet voice.

"Where have I hidden who?" asked the old priest, who was perplexed by Garic's question.

"My Divine Master! Where have you hidden him?"

"Oh!" exclaimed Brother John as a broad smile split his lips. John promptly opened a closet door, unfolded his handkerchief, and gave the old Deacon the other half of the consecrated host. Garic stayed on his knees until there was a knock at the door. He then got up and opened it. Just on the other side of the door stood Gregor.

"Oh, it's you," said Garic as a mischievous twinkle came to his eyes.

"Who is it?" Asked Brother John from the other side of the door.

"It's my brother," said the old Deacon.

"Tell him to get his ugly face in here and say hi to me before I die of old age," said John.

"Now, if anyone else had dared to call Gregor ugly, Garic would have given them a stern talking to. And in his impetuous youth, Garic had often been known to get into brawls when other guys called Gregor ugly. When Brother John did so, however, no one was offended. He told you to go away," said Garic as he tried desperately not to laugh.

"I heard him," said Gregor as he rolled his eyes and pushed Garic out of his way so that he could enter the room.

There is no way of expressing in words the sheer joy on Gregor's face when he saw Brother John standing on the other side of the door waiting to greet him.

The captain of the Palace Guards stooped so that he could fit under Brother John's arm, as he so often did as a boy. The little saintly old monk looked much like a mother hen, tugging her chick under her wing as he lifted his arm to receive Gregor.

"So, little one, your brother tells me that you've been suffering a great deal lately."

"My seizures have returned," said Gregor. "But I am glad though. This is such a dark and dismal world that we're living in, and there's so much sorrow here."

The captain of the palace guards spoke almost in a whisper, hoping that Garic would not hear him.

The reason for Gregor's melancholy mood was that he suddenly remembered the contents of the bag that he had hidden under Garic's bed. Brother John let go of Gregor's shoulders so that he could turn around and pull two stools out from a corner. All three men were quickly seated and started talking.

Since Brother John only had two stools, he sat on the foot of his bed. Well, it really wasn't a bed in the traditional sense of the word. It was simply just a rough plank of wood and it had a heavy woolen blanket draped over it.

When Brother John was seated, Gregor asked, "Are you going to give me the last rights, Father?"

"No," said Brother John sadly. "I can't even give you the Blessed Sacrament. Father Rickmore only gave me a few hosts. I was visited by so many people today that I only had half a host left when your brother came to see me."

Garic suddenly looked guilty. In fact, he looked much like a boy at a birthday party who was caught eating the last piece of cake. Gregor suddenly looked much like the only boy who didn't get a piece of cake, so downcast was his continence.

A faint and mysterious smile came to Brother John's lips as he observed Garic for a moment. Then he asked him, "Do you remember your first Holy Communion?"

"How could I forget?" said the old Deacon. "You were bringing the Blessed Sacrament to a dying old woman in a nearby village."

"I remember that too," said Gregor with a little chuckle, for he suddenly realized why Brother John had no more hosts to give him.

Garic carried on, "Like he was dying when you told him that he would have to wait another year before he received communion."

Father Ivan heard him, and he came to his rescue. He had the Blessed Sacrament hidden on his person. Although nobody told Garic this, he prostrated himself in adoration of his divine Master.

"You accused Father Ivan of taking sides. When you did that, Father Ivan simply responded by saying, "Blessed are the pure of heart, for they shall see God.""

"I got half of that host, and Garic accused me of stealing. He refused to look at me for a whole month afterward because he was so upset with me. That's the first time that I realized that Garic had received a very special grace," said Brother John. "He instantly knows when he comes into the presence of the Blessed Sacrament."

Garic blushed because the conversation started getting rather uncomfortable for him. He tried to excuse himself by bringing up the fact that he had to get ready for the King's banquet that night.

Gregor quickly noticed that Garic was embarrassed, and he came to his rescue by saying, "I had better go as well before they decide to come looking for me."

Gregor headed to the door promptly, and Garic followed him. Before they could leave, though, Brother John stopped them. The old monk handed Garic his little list.

The parchment on which the list was written had a large ink splotch in the center of it. This is because John had dropped his ink pen on it when he was talking to Anetta.

The old priest turned towards Gregor and said, "Thornfield hit Anetta with the door earlier. She wasn't hurt. But it upset me, and I would like you to speak to Thornfield so it doesn't happen again."

When Brother John said this, the captain of the palace guard swung the door wide open. "Who did it?" Asked Gregor quietly as he observed the two soldiers who were standing in the hall, talking to each other. The one on the right said, John. Garic and Gregor then left the room, and Brother John shut the door behind them.

CHAPTER 7

A Man in a Sack

s Gregor walked to where the two soldiers stood, his blood started boiling. Garic was famous for his hot head. However, Gregor certainly had a temper of his own. The old Deacon knew that his brother was furious, and he walked at a safe distance behind him.

As Gregor headed towards Thornfield, he had rage clearly written on his face. Thornfield said the captain of the palace guards in a menacing tone of voice. Thornfield stopped talking to his companion and looked up, but before he could do anything to defend himself, he was punched square in the face by Gregor.

When this happened, the soldier went sprawling across the floor, and he landed on top of a suit of armor with a crash. Gregor went over to where Thornfield was just picking himself up off the floor. Gregor helped the man up roughly by the collar.

"I am Gregor, captain of the Palace Guards. I was told that you hit Lady Anetta with the door. If you ever do that again, or someone so much as complains about you, I will personally string you up by the neck in the King's courtyard. Do I make myself clear?"

Thornfield shook his head, "Yes," vigorously. Gregor then threw him back into the pile of armor. He and Garic tried to make an escape before they got caught by Brother John. The old priest was too quick, however, and he came to his door to see what happened. Garic and Gregor were caught red-handed as they tried to make their retreat.

"Was that really necessary?" asked Brother John with a frown.

"Yes," said Garic and Gregor at the same time, then they turned and left. Right as they turned to go, Brother John opened up the door wide and the two soldiers scurried inside and latched the door frantically behind themselves. It was as if they were afraid that Gregor would come back and string them up in the King's courtyard.

As soon as the door was shut, the sound of singing started coming from Brother John's room. Well, Brother John was singing, but the other two men sounded like dying hounds.

"Divine office," said Garic with a little smile.

"Yeah," said Gregor.

But those two can't Sing. Gregor was in a dark mood, and he still wanted to string Thornfield up for hitting Anetta with the door, and he looked like an angry bear.

As the two brothers walked, Garic put an arm around Gregor's shoulders. Garic was in high spirits, and he broke out into song. He just couldn't help himself. Gregor joined his brother's song. But since he no longer shared Garic's cheery mood, his song wasn't quite as joyous as Garic's was.

The old Deacon drew his song from the Psalms of Praise, while Gregor drew his song from the Psalms of Petition. They chanted their beautiful medley and an old language long forgotten by most people of this day and age, and the sound was a hauntingly beautiful one. A little smile came to Garic's lips as he walked the gorgeous alabaster halls of the King's palace with his brother. *This is just like old times*, thought the old witch hunter.

But the smile quickly faded from his lips when he realized that he would probably never see Gregor again. The last few words of Gregor's song came out sounding like a sob, while Garic somehow managed to stay in tune the whole time. This is despite the fact that he also desperately wanted to weep as well.

When they arrived at the door to Garic's room, the old Deacon let go of his brother's shoulder so that he could open the door. Gregor entered the room first, and Garic followed shortly after him. Garic's room was very small, but it did have a fireplace and a secret passageway that led directly to the stables. This is probably why the High Prince Karegan chose the room for the old Deacon.

Once they entered the room, Gregor collapsed on Garic's chest and wept bitterly. Garic stood there with his back towards his bed while Gregor had his back to the door. Gregor looked like a frightened boy who had been caught in a terrible thunderstorm. And although Garic was the younger of the two brothers, he certainly looked like the older one as he held Gregor's shoulders tightly in an attempt to comfort him. The old Deacon let go of Gregor's shoulders so that he could turn around when he heard someone under the bed sneeze.

"Who's there?" Asked Garic as he drew a cross-hilt sword from its sheath. "Show yourself, or I'll end you swiftly."

The old Deacon had a look of menace about him as he cautiously took a few steps toward the wooden plank that served as a bed for him. The wooden plank jumped a few times, then outrolled a very young man.

"Who are you, boy? And why are you hiding under my bed?" Asked Garic. He spoke in a gruff tone of voice, but in his defense, it wasn't that uncommon for men of his order to be murdered by boy assassins who belonged to this or that coven.

"Well, speak up, boy!" snapped Garic, who was not in a patient mood.

"I, um…" stammered the boy. "Gregor hid me under the bed. He said that I'd be safe from Victor and Larson if I stayed there." A little hopeful smile came to the boy's lips as he spoke.

A perplexed look crossed Garic's face as he sheathed his sword once more. The old Witch hunter crossed his arms over his chest as he turned to face the captain of the palace guards. Gregor suddenly looked sheepish and he started playing with the cuffs of his sleeves nervously when Garic turned to face him.

"Um, brother, why is there a man hiding under my bed?"

"Well," said Gregor as he rubbed his chin thoughtfully. "It's a long, long story!"

"I'm all ears!" Snapped Garic, whose mood was getting worse and worse by the minute.

"I was sent to take Karegan's armor to his room this morning. I thought I was completely alone, so I started singing the Canticle of Daniel at the top of my voice. But I had no idea that this little heathen was waiting just around the corner. He was planning on sticking a poison dagger in me. When he heard me sing, however, he just couldn't go through with his plans. Instead, he had me teach him the Canticle of Daniel. This boy has a sharp wit and an excellent memory." Said the captain of the palace guards.

But he suddenly realized that Garic was tapping his foot impatiently, so he continued his story. "I had to go to the King's secret meeting, so I stuffed the boy into a sack and took him with me."

"Do you mean to tell me that you took this witch assassin to the King's secret meeting?" Asked Garic, who couldn't believe his ears.

"Oh, the king didn't mind. Right after that, I was going to hide him in my room so Victor and Larson wouldn't kill him. My room was being watched by those two thugs, though. So I took him here and sort of forgot about him."

"Seriously, Gregor, you are the only person I know who can literally misplace a whole man under someone else's bed and completely forget about him. What's his name?"

"Oh, I call him Griffey."

"Oh No! Thought Garic," as he buried his face in his hands. "He's giving the boy a nickname. He's getting attached."

Now, the Captain of the Palace Guards looked rough, talked tuff, and put on a mean façade quite easily. But deep down inside, the man was a big bowl of mush. And when he got his heart set on helping someone else, there was no way of deterring him from it.

"Oh, can't he stay here, brother?" pleaded Gregor. "If you send him away, Victor and Larson will just kill him for not doing as he was told. No one says no to their coven without there being dire consequences."

"I am not sure," said Garic as he turned to face the young man again. "Let me see your right hand, boy," said Garic in a stern voice.

When he said this, the boy held out the palm of his right hand to reveal a large pentagram tattoo. When Garic saw this, his face went white, and he shuddered with horror.

"It's too late," said the old Deacon in a grave tone of voice. "He's marked. That means he's killed someone already. He's a criminal." So are we, protested Gregor. Garic put his hands on his hips.

"He's a murderer!" shouted the old Deacon.

"So are we," retorted his brother. "This is my dying wish, Garic. If you love me, you will raise him as if he were your own flesh and blood."

Garic looked like a wet cat as he let his arms fall to his sides once more. The captain of the palace guards had found his brother's soft spot, and he knew it.

"This is dangerous, brother. The boy has been playing with snakes. He could be rabid, but I'll do it," said the old Deacon. Garic spoke almost in a whisper. It was as if he was telling his brother a secret, and he didn't want anyone else to overhear him.

"I'll do it only because it means so much to you, brother! I better go," said Gregor.

No sooner did these words leave his mouth than Garic opened the door and shoved Gregor out into the hallway. The captain of the palace guards chuckled softly when he was shoved out the door by his brother.

"Take a bath and trim your hair and beard. No one will ever believe that Lady Anetta could fall in love with you when you smell like a goat and look like a bear. Oh, and Anetta bites. So be careful not to lose a finger. She sounds like a wild mare I once had."

"Prey tell me, brother, does she also kick?"

"Yes, she does," said Gregor, who was at this point choking back laughter.

After saying this, the Captain of the Palace Guards quickly disappeared down the hall.

Once Gregor was gone, Garic went back into his room and locked the door behind him. As soon as the door was latched, Garic grumbled to himself, just like old times. For almost as long as he could remember Gregor had the habit of adopting pets and then sort of talking Garic into taking care of it for him. Garic was really quite irritated with his brother and maybe even a bit angry.

However, anger quickly gave way to grief, and the old Deacon completely forgot that he wasn't alone as he pressed his forehead against the door and wept without restraint.

"I'm really going to miss that old scoundrel," mumbled the old witch hunter as he got completely lost in his sorrow.

When the young man standing behind Garic made a noise, Garic tried desperately to stop crying as he made an attempt to dry his face on his sleeve. The old Deacon was terribly embarrassed by his show of emotion in front of a complete stranger. He grabbed the hilt of his sword and turned around suddenly when the boy tapped him on the shoulder. Garic let go of his sword, however, when he realized that the boy was only trying to hand him a handkerchief.

Garic stood for a moment and observed the man in front of him before accepting his little gift. The boy was probably in his mid-to-early teens, but malnutrition had stunted his growth. Therefore, the boy could have easily passed for a child of 10. His wavy red hair had been dyed permanently black. His clothes were also all black, like those worn by Victor and Larson. The young man's large green eyes seemed to find wonders everywhere they looked.

As he stood there quietly he observed the witch hunter thoughtfully. Lord Garic was most certainly unlike any other nobleman the boy had ever encountered before. His clothes were in tatters, and there was a smudge of dirt on his trousers because he had been kneeling in the dirt. The man obviously cared very little about his appearance. Garic's eyes were very kind, though, and that was most surprising to the young man who had grown up hearing horror stories about the terror of witches.

After a few moments of awkward silence, the boy said, "You are nothing like they say. I was always told that you were brutish and cruel, but now I realize it was probably just a terrible lie. It does make me wonder, though. Who did you kill?"

"He was a witch," growled Garic. The old Deacon softened his voice though as he added, "He killed my wife. She was very pregnant at the time, and she suffered the most horrible death. After that, I started a religious order of Inquisitors and hunted down most of Deathrogane's coven and executed them publicly in the streets of Merrick."

"You mean you're a witch hunter?" Said the boy.

"No, boy, I mean Inquisitor. We only hunt men guilty of murdering innocent people ritualistically."

"Does that mean you're a priest?" Asked the boy.

"No, said Garic. I'm only a Deacon. However, there are a few priests in my order."

"Is it true that you cut Deathrogane's head off and paraded it through the streets of Merrick?"

"Yes, said the old Deacon. But it was absolutely necessary for me to get my point across. It was necessary but terribly regrettable at the same time. The people of Merrick hailed me as a hero for riding them of the tyrant Deathrogane. They still call me the terror of witches to this day. I was very angry in those days," said Garic sadly.

The boy who was listening intently to Garic had a look of horror on his face. And he asked, "Will you perhaps cut my head off if I anger you?"

"It takes a lot to get me that angry," said Garic.

"Why is your brother Gregor dying?"

"It's your turn to answer questions, boy," said the old Deacon firmly. "First of all, how old are you? What's your name? That is, what do your parents call you? Why do you dye your hair black? And who did you kill? And why did you do it? Oh, and don't lie about your age."

Garic winced when he realized that he had just dumped a heap of questions on the boy. But before he could correct the problem, the young man dove right in and started answering the questions, "First of all…" said the boy. "I hate what they did to my hair. I'm about 15. I was so young when they took me that I can't even remember my parents. Everyone calls me Griffin, except for your brother, of course. He calls me Griffey."

"What do you mean you were so young when you were taken?" Asked Garic with a frown.

"The seven covens take small children when their parents aren't looking. I was gone before my parents even knew it. There were six girls and fourteen boys in my group. The boys and girls live separately under different guardians. What's wrong with your brother Gregor?"

Garic winced when the boy said this. Gregor was right. The boy was terribly clever. And he was really good at dodging questions. "Who did you kill, and why did you do it?" Asked Garic firmly.

This was just about the only question that the boy did not want to answer, and Garic knew it. The old witch hunter stood directly in front of the door and gave Griffin a hard stare. But the young man couldn't bring himself to meet his gaze, and his face went red as he stared intently at the floor.

There was a sudden knock at the door. And Griffin was all too eager to scurry back under the bed because it got him out of answering Garic's question. At least for the time being, that is.

Just on the other side of the door stood Michellie. The man was almost as tall as Dimitri and Malkovich. He had broad shoulders and black hair, which was usually cut short. He had wise dark blue eyes, and his cheeks were sunken, like one who was accustomed to not eating much.

- The palace guard handed Garic a basket of food, and the old Deacon stepped back inside of his room for a moment to set his basket down, but he quickly returned to speak to Michellie.

"What's the food for?" Asked Garic with a little smile.

"Surely, I've not grown that thin. Have I?" Gregor sent it. He thought his pet might be hungry. The old Deacon looked much like a wet cat when Michellie said this.

"Just like old times," murmured Michellie with a little chuckle as he turned to leave.

Garic stopped him, however, and said, "Please send someone to my room with a bathtub, warm water, shears, and a razor."

"Oh, please don't cut your hair and shave!" pleaded Michellie. "That look suits you so well."

"I must look my best tonight, and I've been told that I look like a bear."

"You do," said Michellie. "But it suits you so well!" As Michellie said this, he grinned mischievously as he ducked in order to avoid a playful right hook from Garic. He didn't move quickly enough, though, and his old friend hit him square in the shoulder. The palace guard returned the blow, and Garic was knocked to the floor. Something like this would have normally turned into a playful sort of sparring match between the two old friends, but Michellie saw Lackmore coming out of the corner of his eye, and he bent over Garic under the pretext of helping him up.

But when he did so, he whispered, "Don't let Lackmore see Gregor's little pet if you can help it."

Michellie didn't specify exactly why, but he clearly did not trust Lackmore despite the fact that the two men were close friends.

On the day that Michellie realized that Lackmore had gone astray, he stopped trimming his beard, lost a ton of weight, and took on the appearance of a man who was mourning the loss of a loved one.

This was quite shocking to everyone who knew him because Michellie was a rather handsome man, and he always seemed to take pride in his appearance.

After helping Garic up, Michellie turned and disappeared down the hall with Lackmore. As Michellie walked, he scratched the palm of his hand where there once had been an ugly pentagram tattoo but now there was only a scar to remind him of just how foolish he was in his youth for choosing such a cruel master.

CHAPTER 8

A Cruel Master

fter Michellie left, Garic went back into the room and locked the door behind him. He then said grace over the basket of food before calling Griffin out of his hiding place to eat.

When Griffin came out from under the bed he found that all the food had been laid out for him by Garic. The old Deacon turned his back to the boy and sat at the little writing desk and as he did so, the boy started eating like a heathen.

"Who sent the food?" Asked the boy with his mouthful of apple.

"Who did you kill, and why did you do it?" was Garic's response to this question, and the young man frowned at him. He just wasn't giving up.

Father Ivan used to say that when it comes to stubbornness, there are mulish people, and then there is Garic. Nobody is as stubborn as Garic is, though.

The room went quiet because Griffin was determined not to answer Garic's question at all. All that could be heard for a while was the sound of the boy chewing his food.

After a while, though, there was another knock at the door. Garic went to answer the door while Griffin scrambled back under the bed once more.

Garic swung the door wide open, and in walked abroad maidservant named Brigitte. Right behind her came a train of servants carrying a tub, buckets of water, and many other things for bathing. Just as Brigitte was about to set her bathtub down, Garic had a splendid idea, and he asked her to come back with more water in an hour or so.

When she gave the old Deacon an inquisitive look, Garic exclaimed, "I love taking baths, don't you?" After Garic's declaration of his love for bathing, Brigitte made herself scarce.

Griffin was still hiding under the bed, and he had to hold his breath just to keep from laughing out loud. Once the door was shut, however, he stuck his head out from underneath the bed so that he could mock Garic for being awkward.

"I love taking baths, don't you?" Said Griffin, who was in stitches. "Seriously! You couldn't have thought of anything weirder to say?"

"I should have just told her that I was hiding half of a man under my bed and that he has poor hygiene practices," said Garic.

"Next time just tell her that you smell like a goat and you have to wash twice to get the smell off you. Oh, and I'm not short. I just have a smaller bone structure than most people."

"You are short," said Garic. "You're just an inch shy of being a midget."

As he said this, Garic shoved the boy's head back under the bed. "Now stay there, you little heathen, so that I can have some privacy while I bathe."

"Remember, according to you, I'm just half a man. That would only make me half a heathen," said Griffin with a little smirk.

Garic responded to Griffin's retort by covering his head with a heavy blanket, and the room went blessedly silent. The old Deacon breathed a sigh of relief when this happened because he had grown accustomed to silence since the death of his wife.

When Garic called Griffin out from under the bed, there was a pile of hair on the floor. Garic's black hair was cut short, and his mustache and beard were trimmed back. Griffin was beside himself with excitement over Garic's new look, but the old witch hunter ignored him.

"Here," said Garic as he handed a bar of soap to the young man. "It's your turn to wash the goat smell off of you. Brigitte ran you clean bath water, and it's nice and hot, so you'd better hurry up and bathe."

When Gregor was a boy he often brought Brother John wounded animals to be cared for. The pious old priest would always bathe it before taking it into his hermitage. This was a rite of passage, and Griffin would not be any different than any other wounded critter, which Gregor decided to adopt.

Garic turned his back towards the boy with the intention of laying down between the bed and the wall in order to give him privacy while he bathed. Since Garic didn't have a shirt on, Griffin could clearly see the scars on his back.

"Were you also once in a coven as well?" Asked the boy.

"No, said Garic. Why on earth would you say such a thing?"

"It's just that we both have similar marks on our backs." Garic, who had been lying on his back on the floor behind the bed, sat up for a moment to see what the boy was talking about.

When he did so, Griffin took off his shirt and turned around in order to show the old Deacon the marks on his back. Garic glanced at the boy's back briefly. Then he laid back down again.

Griffin was right about one thing. Garic wasn't cruel, nor was he brutish, and he most certainly was not made of stone either. Once he laid back down on the floor, two large tears rolled down his sunken cheeks.

"Who on earth was capable of doing such a cruel thing?" Wondered the old Deacon as he wiped away his tears with the back of his hand.

Garic was just glad that the boy couldn't see him, though, because the last thing he wanted was to appear soft or weak in front of the boy.

"Who did that to you?" asked Griffin. The boy found a strange sort of delight in the fact that the old Deacon had something in common with him.

"It's still your turn to answer questions," said Garic. "I must know something about you so I can help you get out of the mess you're in. So who did you kill, boy, and why did you do it?"

Garic tried desperately to sound gruff, but despite his best efforts, his voice sounded hoarse and broken, like one who was about to weep. The only sound in the room, which could be heard for a while after that, was the sound of Griffin splashing around in the bathwater.

Finally, after a bit, Griffin broke the silence. Back before I got my tattoo, I had a roommate named Trestan. He was much older than the rest of us when he was taken. Trestan actually remembered his mother. Most of the other boys were jealous of him because of this fact.

"Were you jealous of him?" Asked Garic.

"No! He was like a brother to me, and he was just about the only person who ever showed me kindness. Trestan liked to sing, and I must admit it, he did drive me a little crazy with his love for music, and he would often keep me up at night to teach me a song that his mother had taught him. On the day of initiation, Trestan flatly refused to sign a contract with the Dark Master, and I was told to kill him. When this happened, I told everyone to go to the …… devil. When I defied my coven, I was beaten within an inch of my life, and once I could walk again, I was forced to kill my friend anyway. Trestan had a peaceful and quiet death, but my guardian did not. You can get up now, old man. I'm done bathing, and I have a pair of trousers on."

When Garic got up and turned around, he beheld what appeared to be a flood. I feel as though a cataclysmic event has taken place while I had my back turned towards you.

"Pray tell me where is Noah and his family? Are they OK?" Griffin blinked for a moment at Garic, but when he realized that the old Deacon was just trying to lighten the situation, he said. "I just love taking baths, don't you?"

Garic smiled at the boy's snarky remark, but his smile quickly faded when he realized that Griffin was about to put on his old clothes.

"No!" Shouted Garic as he kicked Griffin's clothes away from him.

"What's your problem?" Asked the boy in frustration as he straightened himself up.

"Look!" Said the old Deacon as he took the boy by the shoulders and gave him a little shake. "You are never again to wear your old Masters' colors. Do you understand me, boy?" Shouted Garic.

"But my hair?" groaned the boy as he brushed his wet hair out of his face with one hand. The old Deacon felt a surge of rage when the boy mentioned his hair. Of course, Garic did notice Griffin's hair the moment he met the boy. But he never before realized the real significance of it.

"Who did that to your hair, child?" Asked Garic in a menacing tone of voice.

"Victor and Larson did it when I killed my guardian the way I did. They said it was because my red hair was too bright for someone who belonged so completely to darkness."

Just as soon as these words left Griffin's mouth, Garic grabbed him by one arm and drug him over to the foot of the bed where he left the shears. The old Deacon started snipping wildly at Griffin's hair.

"Are you angry, old man?" Asked the boy in a worried tone of voice. For you see, he suddenly recalled every horror story he ever heard about Lord Garic, the Terror of witches.

"I'm furious, growled Garic, who was fuming with rage. But not with you, my son. I'm just glad those two criminals are not here."

When Garic was finished cutting Griffin's hair, all that was left was a bit of stubble and a few little cuts to prove that the boy had been through something as horrific as Garic with scissors. Luckily, Griffin still had both ears intact. After cutting Griffin's hair, Garic grabbed his razor and shaved the boy's head clean.

There said Garic, who was obviously very pleased with himself. "Now go burn your clothes child, then come back when you're finished so I can speak to you for a moment before I go."

Griffin did as he was told, but when the old Deacon realized that he was about to touch his old clothes again, he shouted, "Use the poker!

Griffin's clothes went up in flames almost as soon as he threw them on top of the embers of the fireplace. When he was done burning the clothes, he went back to the bed and sat down. Garic pulled up a stool next to the bed and sat down facing the boy.

"Look," said the old Deacon, "Griffin is now dead. He died suddenly when he decided to defy his coven. From now on, you'll be known by a different name. A saint's name. Let me see," said Garic as he rubbed the remnants of his beard thoughtfully.

"We will call you.......... Trestan!" When Garic named the boy's dead friend, he burst out in tears.

"That's not a Saint's name." Protested the boy in between sobs. "Yes, it is," said Garic and a firm voice. "He was a martyr. He preferred death over offending his Divine Master."

This little comment from Garic caused the boy to break out into another fit of violent sobs, but once he composed himself, he said, "It's a beautiful name, and I will do my best to bear it proudly."

Garic got up and put his boots on. He was about to grab his sword and leave. The old Deacon came back, though, and asked, "Trestan, Was there another question you wanted me to answer before I go?"

Trestan blinked at him for a moment, then he said, "Yes. I was wondering who gave you those marks on your back and why?"

"Well…" said Garic, "These marks were a gift from my stepfather, and while he certainly wasn't a wizard, he was a slave to the same cruel master that you once served."

"What do you mean?" Asked the boy.

"Well…" said Garic, "if you step out into the world, you'll find that some people call their master greed. Others call their master lust, pride, envy, etcetera. In the end, they all serve the same cruel master that you once did. The master, which he was a slave to, is called drunkenness. This caused my mother, along with a great deal of other people, a whole lot of pain and sorrow. My stepfather's drunkenness is the reason why my brother Gregor has those terrible scars on his face."

Trestan was full of questions, and Garic did not have time to answer all of them. "How did your wife die?" Asked Trestan.

A sharp pain shot through Garic's soul when the boy mentioned his dead wife, but it was his turn to answer questions, and although he wasn't comfortable discussing his past, neither was the boy.

"Well…" said the old witch hunter, "It all started when the High King of Merrick was assassinated by his uncle, Deathrogane. The Queen of Merrick came riding into our camp with her small child in her arms. Gregor was ready to move mountains to save her and her child. I should have known better, but I also felt compelled to help her. Because I got involved in politics, my wife became a target for Deathrogane and the seven covens. Gregor blames himself for her death. But it wasn't his fault. It was mine. I should have been there that day."

"Where were you?" Asked Trestan curiously.

"I was hunting Ragolon. "Who's Ragolon?"

"Lord Ragolon was the former Captain General of the King's Armies. The man hated me with a passion. It's probably because I took his place when he was sent into exile. My men eventually captured him and cut his head off, but the price I paid for it was unthinkable."

"Are you sure he's dead?" asked the boy.

"Um, they cut his head off! I have never known anyone who survived that," said Garic as he strapped his sword to his hip and headed for the door.

When Trestan saw that Garic was about to leave the room, he begged him not to go.

"Please don't leave me, I'm frightened!" said Trestan with a wide-eyed look of terror on his face. "I am only one of five assassins sent to end the reign of the monarchy in Duchaine and not even I know who the others are. I do know, however, that there are two assassins hiding in the King's banquet hall. They were sent for Lady Anetta. One of the palace guards are supposed to take care of the High Prince Karegan tonight. I know him, but I have no idea what his name is. Did you hear me, old man?" Said the boy when he realized that Garic was still set on going to the King's banquet. "The King's banquet hall is going to be a dangerous place tonight."

Trestan begged and begged, but the old Deacon turn to leave anyway. He was seemingly deaf to Trestan's pleading. As Garic headed for the door, Trestan scurried back underneath the bed. Garic turned back towards the bed once more briefly before leaving the room and he covered the boy's head up with the blanket.

When he did so, Trestan whispered, "I'm frightened."

While the boy only spoke in a whisper, the old Deacon still heard him. A smile came to Garic's lips when Trestan did this because he found it quite difficult to believe that the boy was afraid of anything. After all, Trestan had the gall to defy his coven twice.

Most grown men didn't even have that much courage. As Garic turned the doorknob, Trestan began to sing the song his dead friend had taught him. It was a Psalm of David, and the old Deacon knew it by heart.

"Just don't make too much noise, child, and I'm sure you'll be fine," said Garic right before opening the door.

When he opened the door, he found Michellie just on the other side of it, getting ready to knock. He had what appeared to be a fresh woolen blanket under his arm. But it was really a habit that Brother John had sent for Trestan.

When he noticed the puzzled look on Garic's face, Michellie explained.

"Brother John sent me."

"Oh," said Garic. "Let me introduce you to him. If you just pop in there unannounced, you're likely to frighten the poor fellow half to death." Garic opened the door for Michellie, and then he entered the room himself.

Once they were inside the room, Michellie noticed Trestan's singing from underneath the bed.

"Oh, he does that when he's scared," whispered Garic as he helped Michellie set his arm full of stuff on the small writing desk.

"Come out, child," said Garic in a commanding voice. The tray Brother John had sent for Trestan contained 2 roasted pigeons, fresh bread, a picture of cold milk, and a few other things.

Garic sighed deeply when he suddenly realized that the tray of food was actually the little monk supper. Michellie shot Garic a perturbed look, for he also noticed this.

"Trestan, come out from your hiding place. Repeated Garic patiently. There is someone here I want you to meet."

"Trestan crawled out from underneath the bed. When he saw Michellie, though, he shot Garic a worried glance. He's an old friend, said Garic with a reassuring smile. He is going to protect you from Victor and Larson. You need not worry, child. Said Michellie in his deep voice. Those two are just as frightened of me as they are of Garic. In fact, Brother John actually called Victor into his room and told him that I was to cut his and Larsen's head off if either man felt brave enough to darken Garic's doorway with their shadows. The old Deacon just couldn't help but be a little bit amused by what Brother John had done, and he chuckled softly as he left the room.

Back in the day when Michellie was hunting witches, he had made quite a name for himself, and while Garic was mostly called Terror of Witches, Michellie was simply referred to as the Reaper. Now Brother John knew this, and he was using Michellie's reputation to put fear into Victor and Larson in order to protect Trestan from his old coven.

While the old Deacon walked in the direction of Princess Anetta's bedchambers, he found himself still haunted by the memory of his dead wife. Lady Catalina was long dead, yet Garic could sometimes still smell her perfume, and every now and then, he almost thought he could hear her voice as well. But, of course, this was only the work of the old Deacon's imagination.

When Garic agreed to help the Queen of Merrick, he had no idea what the consequences would be. If he did, Garic probably would not have volunteered himself for the task. But it was these circumstances that forged Garic into the man he was, and he certainly wouldn't have become the witch hunter if it weren't for his tragedy. Garic, who was lost in thought, suddenly found himself standing right outside Lady Anetta's door.

CHAPTER 9

The King's Banquet

When Lady Anetta left Brother John's room, she headed straight for her own bed chambers. As she walked, she pondered what he had told her when he was babbling.

Brother John said that Anetta was destined to be both a queen and a mother and that she had a long life ahead of her. But he also told her to prepare for death. What was he talking about? Was the old mystic speaking in riddles, or was he admonishing her to lead a good life? It was hard to tell.

Upon entering her room, she noticed that someone had left a piece of parchment on her writing desk, which was in the corner of the room by the fireplace. She unfolded the piece of parchment and out rolled a very pretty signet ring. The ring was carved from red jade, and it had three crosses engraved in it.

The note explained that the ring was a relic of sorts and that it was worn for protection. Anetta just assumed that the ring was left there by her father when he realized that she was gone, so she slipped it on a random finger. If she had looked closer at the note, however, she most certainly would not have put the ring on her finger, for it wasn't written in her father's hand at all. In fact, it was actually written by Lord Garic.

This was a sneaky trick which the old Deacon had played on her. But he couldn't think of another way of getting her to wear his signet ring to her father's banquet that night. After she slipped the ring on her finger, Anetta started working out the knots in her hair with a brush. But she soon got help from her maidservants.

Once Anetta was all dressed and her hair was put up in platelets, she left her room.

Standing right outside her door was a rather tall man. He stood about 6 feet tall, and he had a dark olive complexion. His hair was black and curly, and it was just shy of being shoulder-length. He had a short mustache and beard. His features suggested that he was from the East, while his accent suggested that he was from Merrick.

He tried offering Anetta his arm so that he could escort her to the King's banquet hall. However, since she had no idea who the man was, she refused to take his arm until Brigitte stuck her head out of the doorway and said, You can trust him, Angel. He's Gregor's little brother.

Brigitte was a short, brown-skinned woman. She was just as tall as she was wide, and her hair, which had once been very black, was now almost completely silver. She had kind brown eyes and a large mouth.

In spite of her age and her weight, she still managed to be quite pretty. She had a commanding presence, and all the other maidservants called her Mama. She had such a strong personality, in fact, that Gregor once said that if she'd been born a man, she would have made the greatest general the world had ever known. And he wasn't exaggerating either.

Anetta took Garic's arm. Brigitte turned and disappeared down the hall along with her other maidservants who had helped Anetta dress for the night's festivities.

As the old maidservant sauntered down the hall, the younger maidservants followed shortly behind her, and Brigitte looked much like a mother duck with a brood of ducklings trailing after her. Anetta tripped over her own feet after taking three steps, and if Garic wasn't holding on to her, she probably would have fallen flat on her face.

When Anetta caught her balance once again, she freed her arm from Garic so that she could turn around and face him. She put one hand over her mouth as she gasped, "You're the wild man I threw out of the arena this morning."

Then, all of a sudden, a sad sort of expression crossed her face as she said, "I'm sorry, Lord Garic! I would never have done that if I had known who you really were."

"That's Okay," said Garic with a broad and mischievous grin. "I must admit it, watching you mop the floor with those two scoundrels was good for my soul. Especially since your father has granted Victor and Larson diplomatic immunity in order to prevent a war with Merrick. I can't even arrest them and bring them to justice. I am so pleased with you, my lady. In fact, I could dance around you like a maypole."

Anetta frowned at Garic for a moment or so before taking his arm once more, and they continued on their way towards the banquet hall.

Garic had originally planned on executing both Victor and Larson as soon as they left King Ruben's Palace because they would no longer have diplomatic immunity. This was on account of the damage the two men had been causing the people of Duchaine.

Brother John, however, made Garic take a vow of peace. That is, the pious old priest had refused to give him the other half of his consecrated host until Garic vowed not to harm Victor or Larson unless, of course, he was defending himself or Lady Anetta.

This was spiritual blackmail. However, Garic was easily coerced into complying with Brother John's condition for receiving the Blessed

Sacrament. The Old Deacon knew full well that Brother John only did this for his own good. John promised that the Divine Master would send someone else to execute the two murderers.

Garic had his hands tied anyway when he had agreed to take Lady Anetta to a convent. It wasn't like Garic was in the wrong for wanting to execute the two Wizards, though. In fact, Garic's main job description was hunting down witches guilty of murdering innocent people ritualistically and executing them.

However, the old Deacon had gotten too close to his work over the past few years, and executing Victor and Larson would have been spiritually harmful for Garic. Anetta and the old Deacon walked arm in arm until they came to a small door which was just a bit ajar.

Anetta then let go of Garic's arm and said, "Wait here. I'll be back shortly. There is something I must do. It won't take long, though, I promise." She then disappeared into the room.

Just inside the room stood her mother. The Queen was standing and talking to the head cook. Anetta kissed her on the cheek and said, "I love you, mother," then scurried away, back out the door from which she came.

She didn't see it because she left so quickly, but when she kissed her mother on the cheek, the Queen's eyes filled with tears. It had been a long time since Anetta and her mother had anything kind to say to each other.

When she finally made it back to where Garic was waiting for her, tears were streaming down Anetta's cheeks. Garic struggled for a moment or two before he produced the snow-white handkerchief from his pocket. He then offered it to Anetta, who took it and thanked him.

Garic asked, "Are you OK? Has someone threatened you, my lady? If someone has hurt you, I will end them."

As he said that, he grabbed the hilt of his sword, and for a moment, Anetta could have easily imagined him as Captain General of the King's armies. Garic, who usually had such a sweet and gentle demeanor, suddenly appeared menacing as he grabbed his sword.

"No one has hurt me. I merely said hello to my mother, and we rarely speak to each other. Garic let go of the hilt of his sword and offered Anetta his arm once again.

"Women are odd creatures." Murmured Garic under his breath as Anetta took his arm once again. Anetta heard him, and she raised an eyebrow at the old Deacon.

When Lady Anetta and Lord Garic entered the King's great banquet hall, arm and arm, they certainly looked like a couple. They were both dressed in blue silk, which looked even more luxurious in the dim Light of the King's great banquet hall. Although their clothes were different shades of blue, they still sort of matched, and Garic's signet ring on Anetta's hand must have spoken volumes, at least to some people in the King's banquet hall that night.

The King's great banquet hall had a tall ceiling which was supported by great oak beams, and there were two enormous hearths on either side of the room and they gave warmth and light to the King's guests. There were several smaller rectangular tables scattered around the room, and in the center of the room stood the King's great table. The King's table was in the shape of a long rectangle.

The King of Duchaine always sat at the head of this table with his queen on one side and the Crown Prince on the other one. The rest of the table was reserved for members of the royal family and traveling dignitaries.

Anetta sat at the foot of the table with Garic on her right side, and the place to her left was vacant. King Dinithall tried to sit there, but the High Prince Karegan was too quick, and he took the vacant place next to his twin sister long before the old King of Merrick could.

Now Prince Karegan preferred to sit next to his parents, however, he knew that Anetta probably had a dagger hidden on her person somewhere. If King Dinithall decided to try anything cute, he would surely get stabbed by his sister. Since that was the last thing that the High Prince wanted to happen at his father's banquet, he sat next to his sister.

Right next to him sat Dimitri and Malkovich, shoulder to shoulder. The King's table quickly filled up with Karegan's friends. Soon, there were only a few places left for King Dinithall, Victor, and Larson to sit. Infact, the only places left for them were the places which were usually occupied by the High Prince and his two bodyguards. Garic and Karegan both stood up and gripped the hilt of their swords tightly when King Dinithall came to take the place next to Anetta. Victor and Larson were standing right behind him, and they quickly scurried to their places at the table. It was as though they were afraid that their amnesty would quickly run out, and they were going to lose their heads in the middle of the King's banquet hall.

The king of Merrick, on the other hand, kept his composure quite well as he walked to the head of the table. And he quietly seated himself next to King Ruben. The only indication that he was nervous was the fact that he kept rubbing the palms of his hands together. This was probably because King Ruben grabbed the hilt of his sword when the old king of Merrick joined him at the table, but he did not stand up though. He just scowled at King Dinithall.

King Ruben made his point quite clearly, though, and it was obvious to everyone present that King Dinithall was an unwelcome guest in Duchaine. Everyone was simply too polite to say it out loud. When Victor went to his seat at the table, he made Larson move over and his companion was forced to sit next to a member of Garic's order of Inquisitors.

This man's name was Lord Roslyn, and he was about the same age as the High Prince Karegan was. Rosalyn made Larson uneasy, but there was very little he could do about it, especially since Victor ranked higher in the coven than he did. This often meant that Larson got bullied by Victor and, in this case, pushed in front of the carriage.

When Lord Roslyn suddenly realized that he made Victor and Larson nervous, a look of delight came to his face, and as the edge of his mouth curled up in a little smile, he looked much like a cat playing with mice while Victor and Larson looked very much like frightened mice.

Rosalyn played with the hilt of his sword, and his dark gray eyes twinkled with mirth as he did so, for he realized that this made Victor and Larson even more uneasy than before. In fact, the two men were literally breaking out in a cold sweat.

Lord Rosalyn clearly got his jollies out of observing the discomfort which he was causing them. The captain of the palace guards had disarmed both Victor and Larson before they entered the King's great banquet hall, and they were the only ones at the King's table who had no weapons of their own.

In fact, even the king of Merrick was allowed to wear a small, short sort of dagger. This was a staghorn dagger which was often worn by kings on special occasions. Victor and Larson, on the other hand, weren't even allowed that much.

Shortly after, the High Prince was seated at the table he was joined by a beautiful young woman. Malkovich got up and gave the Lady Ella his place next to the High Prince. Karegan didn't recognize her, though, until she spoke to him.

"I'm sorry, I'm just a little late," said the young lady timidly.

"Oh, no, I believe you're just in time," said the High Prince Karegan with a little smile.

Karegan breathed a sigh of relief when Ella's stepmother and stepsister were intercepted by a palace guard. The man took them to a table in the back of the room. Camilla was livid with rage but there was nothing that she could do about the situation except for acting exceedingly haughty, and that she did incredibly well.

"My dear, said the High Prince. I believe you're just in time. I truly appreciate you being here. The last thing I wanted was to sit next to your sister Jezebel, she can't seem to find a modest dress to wear."

Although Karegan neglected to say it, the neckline on Jezebel's dress that night was so low that her breasts were hardly staying inside of her gown.

About halfway through the meal, King Ruben of Duchene stood up to make an announcement. Everyone in the room stood with the king of Duchaine.

"I am pleased to announce the engagement of my beloved daughter Anetta to our dear friend Lord Garic." And he added, "There is no one in this world that I trust more than this man, and I know I will not be disappointed in him." It was as if the old king was saying, *Don't mess this up,* Garic. At least, that is how it sounded in Garic's ears.

A hush fell about the room for a moment, but the silence was soon broken by Karegan, who proposed a toast to the beautiful new couple. Just as he did this, Garic emptied his goblet of wine almost in one swallow and then nearly choked on it. "Congratulations," shouted Dimitri and Malkovich as they raised their goblets of wine.

"Hurray for the beautiful new couple." Shouted Rosalyn, and he was echoed by several of the palace guards.

Anetta was livid with rage when her engagement was announced by her father, and she struggled in vain to get Garic's signet ring off her little fat finger. When Garic realized what she was doing, he grabbed her by the wrist and raised her hand high in the air so that everyone in the King's great banquet hall could see his ring on her finger. He then let go of Anetta's wrist.

As he did so, he whispered, "Keep it on your hand, woman, Or so help me!"

Anetta looked like she wanted to stab Garic. She stopped tugging at his ring, though. The applause spread throughout the room until everyone was clapping except for the King of Merrick, Victor Larson, and Anetta, of course.

"But he's a Deacon…" protested Larson in a loud voice. That was the last thing that he said, though, because Lord Rosalyn whispered a threat in his ear while gripping the hilt of his sword tightly. This isn't good! Murmured Victor under his breath.

Now, the plan was to take Anetta back to Merrick under the grounds that she was King Dinithall's concubine, and Doomlock would finish his ritual on her there, and he would become the most powerful wizard in the Seven Covens. But just in case something was to go wrong, there were two assassins hiding under the King's table.

Anetta getting engaged to a powerful Lord was bad news. They did expect King Ruben to cook something up, though, in an effort to save his daughter. The fact that this man was the terror of witches himself was positively the best imaginable counter-move.

Since Anetta was now officially engaged, there was no lawful way to take her back to Merrick with King Dinithall. Of course, they could just kill her fiancée and abduct her. Killing Garic was almost impossible, and if either Victor or Larson were caught signaling the assassins who killed Lady Anetta that night, well, let's just say their amnesty would run out quickly.

If Anetta survived the night, however, and she went to produce an heir to the throne of Duchaine with the old witch hunter, then Doomlock would be terribly displeased. When Doomlock became displeased, people around him tended to die. Because Victor was feeling quite mortal, he decided to signal the assassins. The signal was supposed to be something falling on the floor.

Victor had originally planned on dropping his goblet of wine, but he suddenly realized that this would be far too obvious. So he tipped his chair over instead. He tried to be inconspicuous, but the old witch hunter was instantly onto him. When Victor's beautiful mahogany chair hit the floor, Garic threw himself to the ground.

Since the old Deacon grabbed Anetta and Karegan, all three of them went sprawling across the floor on their backs. Neither Garic nor Karegan were able to draw their swords before a man came at Anetta with a poisoned dagger. But she produced a dagger of her own, though, and flung it at the assassin.

When Anetta did so, Karegan murmured, "I knew she had a dagger hidden somewhere."

The man dodged her blade, and while the dagger missed its mark, it did hit the assassin in the shoulder though. The room was still echoing with applause when Victor's chair hit the floor, but when Anetta threw her dagger, the whole room went quiet. It was so quiet, in fact, that you could almost hear crickets.

Malkovich went to look for Victor and Larson, but neither one could be found, for they quickly made themselves scarce. The stark silence of the room was broken by King Ruben when he announced that everyone should join the newly engaged couple on the dance floor.

After this, everyone started to head towards the dance floor. "Come dance with me," whispered Garic as he helped Anetta off the floor.

"Drop dead," growled Anetta under her breath.

"Your father has announced that we are going to dance," whispered Garic. And he added, there's another assassin hiding somewhere in this room, and he's probably lurking under our table. That makes the dancefloor the safest place.

Anetta didn't want to make a scene, so she said nothing. She simply just stood there and gave the old Deacon a dirty look. I know that look, thought the High Prince as he left his father's banquet hall. He smiled because he knew full well that Garic was going to have a whole lot of trouble getting Anetta to cooperate with him when she had that expression on her face.

It didn't take long for Garic to realize that Anetta had no intention on going to the dance floor with him. So he Simply put her in an arm lock and made her come with him anyway.

"I beg your pardon, my lady, but I have sworn to protect you, and you'll be in grave danger if you remain here." It took a series of arm locks to get Anetta to the dance floor, and it took even more to get her to move her feet.

Once they were on the dance floor, a small group of musicians started playing a lively tune. Garic and Anetta spun around the dance floor wildly. What they did, however, did not resemble dancing in the least bit. In fact, it rather looked like a sparring match.

The two got a whole lot of dirty looks from other couples because they kept bumping into people on the dance floor. "Wow, this is exciting," whispered Garic just before he ducked a blow from Anetta's elbow.

About halfway through the dance, however, Garic had his fill of Anetta's violence, and he desperately wanted to leave her on the dance floor, but she would not have been safe if he did so. So, it certainly wasn't an option. Garic breathed a sigh of relief when he saw Brother John approaching.

As soon as Brother John was close enough, Garic flung Anetta at him and said, "Keep it safe for me, Father, while I'm gone." Garic turned to leave, but after taking a few steps, he stopped and turned around for a moment.

"I will meet you in my room in a bit. I will bring tea for everyone, but first, I must go speak to someone for a moment." Garic then disappeared, and Brother John offered Anetta his arm and she gladly took it. He then escorted her off the edge of the dance floor and out of the King's banquet hall. Lord Rosalyn followed shortly behind to ensure the safety of Princess Anetta. "Is there something wrong, my dear?" asked Brother John, who suddenly realized that Anetta was fuming with anger.

"Yes," growled Anetta. "Garic tricked me into wearing his signet ring, and then he forced me to dance with him. People used to call me King Dinithall's mistress, but now I will also be known as the woman who got engaged to a Deacon. I will have a reputation worse than that of Mary of Magdalene."

"You must really forgive Lord Garic's barbaric behavior," said Brother John. "The man hardly knew his mother. In fact, he was raised by two heathens living as hermits in the mountains. Although what Garic did was regrettably inappropriate, you can rest assured that he only had your best interests at heart. And besides, put in..." Lord Rosalyn with a devious grin. "Nobody who saw you, too, on the dance floor tonight would ever believe that you were actually engaged. In fact, I don't even think they call that dancing."

"No," said Brother John with a mischievous twinkle in his eye.

"They call that trying to stay alive when your dance partner wants to stab you with her dagger."

"Well," said Brother John, "I completely understand why you are so angry, my dear. Just don't let the sun go down on your anger child."

"The sun is already down," said Anetta. "So I can be angry with him until tomorrow."

"Very well," said Brother John ."But Garic is most likely to do something far worse tomorrow, and you'll be even more upset with him then."

Anetta laughed because she thought that Brother John was just joking. However, he most certainly was not.

CHAPTER 10

Gregor's Bedside

fter Garic and Anetta left for the dance floor, Lackmore came and got his sister Ella. The palace guard took her to Garic's room so that Michellie could keep her safe while he found someone who could take her home.

As they walked towards Garic's room, they talked, and Lackmore was chock full of questions.

"First of all, I would like to know how on earth you got mother to let you come tonight?"

"She said I could come if I finished my chores and picked up some shards of a broken plate. She also said that I had to find my own way here. So, I borrowed a donkey from our neighbor. When I got here, I felt ashamed of my appearance, though, because I was still wearing rags. A servant named Brigitte met me just as I was about to leave the stables. She was sent by Brother John to get me ready for the King's banquet tonight. Brigitte fixed my hair and put me in one of Anetta's silk dresses."

"Broken plate, huh?" said Lackmore as he rubbed his chin thoughtfully. "So Mother is still playing at that game, is she? You know, she curses those, Ella, when she wants to leave you home. It's supposed to be impossible to pick them up. So, how on earth did you manage it. You remember the first time Mother did that?"

"When I tried sweeping them up with a broom, they slid across the floor. It was as if they had a mind of their own. So I picked them up with my bare hands. That was a terrible mistake because my hands got cut up so badly. In fact, no amount of binding my hands stopped them from bleeding. Mother gave in to me that time and I was allowed to come to mass with her. I was in so much pain when I walked through the doors of the Great Cathedral, however, that I wished I had never asked to come. Out of nowhere came the High Prince Karegan. He took me by the wrist and dipped my hands in holy water. As soon as my hands hit the water, all my cuts disappeared. The High Prince then handed me two jars. One of them contained Epiphany water, and the other one contained exercise salt. After that day, I have had very little trouble with Mother's cursed plates or anything else for that matter. Oh Ella, sometimes I just wish that you'd give in to mother and join our...."

Lackmore stopped in the middle of his sentence because Ella suddenly quit walking and pulled her arm away from him so that she could turn around and confront him.

Ella said nothing, she just stood there, staring at Lackmore with an indignant expression on her face. Her angry blue eyes flashed furiously as she quietly dared Lackmore to finish his sentence.

"Sorry, sis," said Lackmore. For once, he actually managed to make his booming voice sound soft and gentle. Ella unfolded her arms so that she could remove a stubborn golden lock from her face and tuck it behind her ear. As she did so, she sighed. Ella had already heard every argument in the book from her brother.

"You don't know how the world works, everyone is doing it, and You don't know what's good for you." She even got the, *You think you're better than everyone else*, speech from him.

However, this only got a pair of wooden clogs thrown at his head. Ella missed, of course, however, the impression the clogs had left on her brother was a lasting one.

"I guess I'll forgive you this time," said Ella as she once again took Lackmore's arm so that he could continue to escort her.

"Next time, however, I will punish you by making you lick the floor though." Lackmore stumbled when Ella said this.

"That's a cruel and unusual punishment, don't you think?" Said Lackmore with a chuckle. "Where on earth do you get these ideas anyways?"

"Oh, I got the idea from the little wager Karegan had with Lord Gregor."

"That man is a terrible influence on you, sis, and you are never to speak to him again." Said Lackmore, who was obviously just joking.

"Well, he's your friend," said Ella with a little smile. "Perhaps you're keeping company with bad people." She only meant this as a joke as well, but it hit just a little too close to home for Lackmore.

"We may disagree about a lot of things, but I love you dearly, and I would willingly lay down my life to protect you." It was Ella's turn to stumble this time, and she murmured something under her breath.

Now Lackmore wasn't quite sure what she said. However, he thought that she made some sort of reference to a donkey. But of course, Ella would never have called her brother an ass, so Lackmore was sure that he was just mistaken.

Ella lost her mother at birth, so she had no memory of her. The girl was only three when her father married again, and shortly after her father's second marriage, Lackmore was born. Ella's stepmother seemed to have no concept of discipline, and her father was often ill due to heart problems, so Ella usually looked after her brother. She oftentimes doled out punishment to him as well.

Now, Lackmore eventually grew out of spankings however, there have been a few times when Ella had thought that perhaps a thorough spanking would do him a great deal of good.

The two eventually came to Garic's door. Lackmore knocked on it, and Michellie's deep voice answered him from the other side of the door.

"It's me, Lackmore. I have come to hide my sister Ella with you."

"Oh," Said Michellie as he quickly opened the door to let Ella into the room. But since Lackmore insisted on lingering in the hallway, Michellie grabbed him by the arm and yanked him inside the room as well.

"Get in here, you thug," Said Michellie as he pulled Lackmore into the room. As soon as Lackmore was inside the room, Michellie locked the door frantically. It was as if he was afraid that some invisible danger was lurking just outside the room.

Once Lackmore was inside of Garic's room, he noticed the captain of the palace guards lying on what passed as a bed for Garic and his breastplate and helmet were lying on the floor near the foot of the bed.

Trestan sat beside Gregor, and he was weeping like a boy who was about to lose his father. The boy was wearing one of Brother John's habits, and since he was wearing his hood down to hide the fact that he was weeping, Lackmore did not recognize him at first. But he recognized Lackmore quickly. If it had been anyone else lying on the bed, Lackmore would have probably cracked some inappropriate joke about the man having too much to drink.

However, since Lackmore had a great deal of respect for his captain, he said nothing. When Trestan noticed Lackmore, he stopped crying. The boy stood, and his hood fell off his head.

"Look, if you have come to kill me, take me outside. I deserve to die for what I have done. I'll come quietly. Only let my friends go. They're innocent."

"Be quiet, you foolish boy." Snapped Lackmore, who suddenly recognized the young man who was wearing Brother John's habit. We're about to both be standing in the same hot water.

When Michellie realized that Trestan and Lackmore knew each other, he seized the hilt of his sword. It was as if he was about to end the life of his fellow palace guard, but he suddenly realized that Lackmore was also in trouble, and he let go of his sword. He was about to lecture the young palace guard when Brother John knocked on the door. Lackmore was really eager to let John in because it saved him from Michellie's lecture.

The door was opened at once by Lackmore, and Brother John entered the room. Right behind him came Anetta and Lord Rosalyn. As soon as Anetta stepped through the doorway, she noticed Gregor lying on the bed, and she was filled with alarm.

"What happened?" Asked Anetta as she rushed to Gregor's bedside. She was obviously talking to Brother John. But instead of answering her question, the old priest turned to Lackmore and said, "Leave us."

He then added in a quiet tone of voice, "I will personally make sure that your sister gets home safely."

Lackmore left the room, but not before saying goodbye to Ella. He gave his sister a kiss on the forehead. When he did so, two large tears rolled down Ella's cheeks, for she knew full well that she would never see her brother alive again.

Michellie turned to leave as well, but on his way out, Brother John grabbed him by the sleeve and whispered, "You may trim your beard and hair now, my son. He's come back."

Now Michellie hadn't done so since he realized that Lackmore had gone astray and his appearance was even more wild than that of Garic. Once Michellie left, John shut the door behind him.

Brother John turned to Anetta and answered her question just as soon as the door was latched. Gregor got upset and had one of his fits, "When I told him that he could not come with you and Garic tonight. Sorry, my lady, but you must go without him. Your friend is too sick to come with you, and he'll just slow you and Garic down."

"Who said I'm going anywhere with Garic?!" Growled Anetta indignantly.

"But my lady," protested Brother John, "you must leave before dawn breaks tomorrow, or you will surely die."

"I'm not leaving Gregor when he's like this, said Anetta. He would do the same for me."

"That's different, protested Brother John. Lord Doomlock wants you dead, child. If you stay here, you will not only get killed yourself, but others will also die to protect you."

Anetta didn't respond to Brother John's argument. She just sat there and gave him a sort of stubborn look. It wasn't that she was being selfish though. She simply had a very difficult day, and she was no longer thinking straight. Garic came to the door soon after this.

The High Prince Karegan and his two bodyguards were with him. Brigitte had also come. She insisted on coming along so that she could carry things. She really just wanted an excuse to check on Gregor, though, so that she could make sure he was ok.

"Open up," said Garic without even knocking at the door. It was quickly opened by Rosalyn.

Brother John and Lord Rosalyn stepped outside the room for a moment in order to help Garic and Brigitte with their armfuls of stuff. When Brother John realized that Karegan was the only person who was not carrying anything, he accused the young Prince of being a arrogant snob. Since Garic refused to let Karegan carry anything, the old Deacon tried to come to Karegan's rescue. However, Brother John gave Garic a little wink followed by a mischievous smile. Only Garic saw this, and it was enough to silence him. Karegan's face went seven shades of red when he was reproached by Brother John. He quickly forgot all about his embarrassment, though, when he saw Gregor lying on the bed.

"What happened?" Asked Karegan in dismay.

"He just had a seizure, baby," said Brigitte. "He'll be okay."

The old maidservant quickly put down her arm full of stuff so that she could check Gregor's pulse. She then turned to leave, but as she did so, she said. "Father, make sure this child gets home safely."

Brother John shut and bolted the door behind her. After he did so, he turned to Garic and said, "I need Lord Rosalyn to bring Lady Ella home before midnight." Garic gave Lord Rosalyn a quiet nod of the head, and the young man headed promptly to the door. He stopped, however, when he realized that Lady Ella did not follow him. And he asked, "What's wrong, my dear?"

"I am still wearing Anetta's dress, and I must change before I leave," said Ella.

"Keep it," said Anetta. "You look better in it than I do, anyways."

Ella was excited to have a dress that wasn't completely threadbare. Anetta was quite amused by Ella's reaction, and she smiled as she watched her leave the room wearing her favorite Crimson silk dress.

Lady Ella followed Lord Rosalyn to the king's stables. The man insisted that she ride a horse back to her mother's cottage. The little donkey was returned to his owner by a palace guard named Arlo.

When she finally made it to the little cottage and Ella approached the door of her home, she finally felt safe. But Ella had no idea that Lord Doomlock was waiting just around the corner for her.

CHAPTER 11

Gregor's Tea

 urry up and drink your tea, my lady," said Garic as he took a tray of tea cups to the bed where Gregor lay sleeping. Anetta looked like a wet cat, and she refused to even acknowledge Garic's presence in the room.

"She's not coming with you," said John with a frown.

The old priest frowned because he noticed that Anetta was reaching for Gregor's cup and not the one intended for her. But the look on Garic's face begged the old priest not to say a word, so Brother John remained silent despite his better judgment. There was nothing in this world that Anetta hated more than cold tea, so she emptied her cup quickly.

Once she had finished her tea, she asked, "Who on earth made this, and why is there so much honey in it?"

"That, my dear, is called rot root tea. It has a lot of honey in it because that's the only way to make it palatable because it's so bitter. It was intended for my brother Gregor to help him sleep. But it will also work marvelously on you, my dear." As Garic said this, Anetta slipped out of consciousness, and she would have slid to the floor at the foot of the bed if Karegan did not catch her.

"You're going to have a quiet ride into the mountains," said Karegan with a broad smile just as devious as the one on Garic's face.

A look of horror crossed Brother John's face as he watched Garic stuff Princess Anetta into the same sack which once held Trestan. And since no one ever taught the boy good hygiene practices, the sack reeked like a smelly teenage boy.

"Oh, she'll get used to the smell after a while." Said Garic when he noticed the look on Brother John's face.

Trestan was about to open the door when the howls of wolves were heard just outside the room, and his face was suddenly filled with fear as he said, "Those are no ordinary wolves. They have finally come for me," groaned the boy as he rubbed his hands together nervously.

"Werewolves," said Karegan, almost in a whisper.

"Spirit wolves," said Garic as his face also went white with terror.

The devil corrected Brother John blandly as he vested himself for mass. John grumbled for a few moments under his breath when he realized that someone had carelessly stuffed the vestments in a sack, and they were now terribly wrinkled.

Garic stood staring at the door, trying desperately to figure out a solution to his problem, while Dimitri and Malkovich made themselves busy transforming the little writing desk into a makeshift altar.

Karegan went crawling around on the floor on his hands and knees in search of a lever that would open a secret passageway, and when he found what he was looking for, he let out a triumphant cry of joy. Karegan pulled the lever, and a hole opened up in the wall.

"Take this way," said the High Prince Karegan. "It's the safest way." When the boy realized that he was going to have to leave the room with Garic while he was being hunted by spirit wolves, he hid his face in Brother John's vestments as he whispered, "I'm scared."

"My son, you have deceived me. You had me believing that your not afraid of anything. Look, I want you to go with Garic tonight. He's not a very nice person, but he's one of the best men I've ever had the pleasure of calling friend. I'm sure that he will try your patience at times. But I'm equally as sure that he will protect you with his life."

After being reassured by Brother John, Trestan turned around and disappeared through the secret passageway. Garic knelt for Brother John's blessing before following the boy. But the little old priest crossed his arms over his chest and scowled at him. After a few moments, though, he did give his blessing to the old witch hunter.

Brother John's blessing was a rather odd one, though. And it caused Karegan to laugh hysterically. This was probably because Brother John begged the Divine Master to bless and keep Garic out of childish mischief. And while John did speak in an old language, Both Karegan and Garic understood what he said perfectly.

After receiving Brother John's blessing, Garic slung his sack over one shoulder. But he paused for a moment to stare at the motionless figure of Gregor lying on the bed. It was as if he was saying goodbye to his Big Brother for the very last time. Karegan noticed this, and his eyes filled with tears, for he understood full well what it is like to lose a brother.

Karegan gave the old Deacon a one-armed hug in an effort to comfort him. Garic put down his sack for a moment so he could respond to the High Prince Kerrigan. This was not the obnoxious headlock as before, but rather, it was truly the embrace of a father.

"Goodbye, my son," Whispered Garic. He then picked up his sack once more and disappeared into the darkness.

Trestan had already gone and the old witch hunter had to move fast if he was to catch up with the young man. The noise at the door got louder and louder. As Garic disappeared down the dark corridor of the secret passageway, Karegan whispered, Goodbye, my old friend. The young Prince then pulled the lever again and the hole in the wall closed up once more.

As he pulled the lever, the High Prince Karegan frowned because he suddenly realized that Garic had somehow managed to slip his signet ring off his finger. It was no wonder that the old witch hunter had once been dubbed Prince of Thieves, for this man truly had sticky fingers. Brother John started saying Mass after Garic left, and the howls, along with the scratching noises at the door, ceased the instant the pious old priest pronounced the words of consecration.

Dawn seemed to come quickly, as it often does for those who neglect to sleep at night. Brother John went to the King's dungeon as soon as the sun rose that day in the hopes of bringing the Blessed Sacraments to the two assassins who had been apprehended the night before.

The old Priest hoped to reach the criminals before they were sent to the gallows for their crimes. While he was gone, the High Prince Karegan and his two bodyguards wrapped themselves in their cloaks and laid down on the floor near the fireplace to rest so that they could keep an eye on Gregor.

Karegan, however, did not sleep because he had a troublesome vision. In his vision, the High Prince saw the death of the two assassins. While Brother John walked in the direction of the cell in which the two men were kept, he suddenly had a vision of his own. The pious old priest was forced to sit down while his vision lasted on account of his site failing him.

This often happened when he had one of his visions. Brother John was forced to sit down in the middle of a flight of steps so he wouldn't fall and hurt himself. Once the vision was over and his sight returned, the old mystic got up and went in search of a lost soul. It wasn't long before John bumped into Lord Lackmore, and the old Priest knew instantly that this was the lost soul whom he sought. Brother John stood and observed Lackmore and his companion, who stood before him.

Lackmore had brown hair and dark eyes. His facial hair had not yet come in, so he only had a wispy sort of Peach fuzz on his face. Lackmore was incredibly tall and stalky. His companions name was Drago. And he was tall and stalky as well. He had black hair and hazel eyes. Both men would probably be considered quite ordinary in appearance by most people.

Drago's helmet and breastplate shone in the dim light of the room, while Lackmore, on the other hand, wasn't wearing his uniform at all. In fact, the palace guard appeared to have simply gotten out of bed, thrown on a pair of trousers and boots, and headed straight for the King's Dungeon so that he could interrogate the prisoners. Lackmore was holding a candle while Drago was holding a hot poker.

"Where are you going with that ugly thing?" Asked Brother John in a stern voice.

"We are going to interrogate the prisoners," said Lackmore boldly in his booming voice. "But why are you here, father?"

"I'm looking for a lost soul," said Brother John in such a way that the two men suddenly looked remorseful.

They looked like two boys caught red-handed torturing a cat, and Brother John looked much like a stern adult who had caught them at it. "Leave us," Drago said Brother John in a commanding voice. "I will deal with you later!" He added as he snatched the poker away from the man.

Drago sauntered off into the darkness and left the pious old priest alone with Lackmore. When John was sure that he was alone with the palace guard, he began to speak to Lackmore.

"Oh, foolish boy, didn't your mother teach you not to play with snakes?" Said Brother John.

"Old man," said Lackmore. "You've been drinking too much Sacramental wine, and now you're talking nonsense."

Brother John's eyes flashed with angry indignance when he was accused of being a drunk. John sat the poker in the corner, put both hands on Lackmore's collar, and ripped his fine linen shirt almost completely down the front, thus exposing the ugly pentagram tattoo on the chest of the palace guard.

When Brother John did this, Lackmore's face went white with terror because he recalled all the tales told about Brother John. "The Mystic who could read souls. *They're all true,*" thought the palace guard. "And now I'm doomed to the gallows."

Brother John, who suddenly realized that Lackmore was frightened by him, softened the tone of his voice as he continued to speak to him.

"Look, my son said the old monk. That poker is still hot enough to give you a marvelous burn. And it would take that hideous mark of rebellion clean off your chest. We are All alone. Let me help you. After that mark is gone, I'll hear your confession. No one has to know this. It will be our little secret, and God is the only other person aside from us who will be aware of it.

Brother John, at this point, was so sad that you couldn't even look at him without wanting to weep. Lackmore was feeling very, very guilty, and he could no longer bring himself to meet the gaze of the little priest.

"Now, I'm not sure why this is so, but oftentimes, when people feel guilty, and they come across mercy, they flee."

That is exactly what Lackmore tried to do. But John was not about to let him escape that easily. The palace guard made a dash for the exit, but John was too quick though and he grabbed him by the wrist before he could get away. The palace guard struggled desperately to escape, but it was of no use, and he knew it because Brother John had him in a death grip.

After a moment or so, Lackmore quit struggling and resigned himself to his defeat. He just stood there in front of the little old priest, staring at the floor with a look of belligerence mixed with guilt on his face.

"Look," said Brother John. "You never know when death may come to you, my son. Please clear your soul while there is time. Life is short. It often is as fleeting as a cloud of smoke and a stiff breeze, and death too often comes like a thief in the night when you least expect it." Brother John's voice had gone from gentle and sad to heart-rending. In fact, his tone of voice had become so sad that it would make you weep if you could hear it.

His last few words came out sounding like a sob, but Lackmore appeared to be completely unmoved. Brother John was not about to give up on him, though, and he reached inside his habit and pulled out a two-inch crucifix.

"Take this, said Brother John as he broke the cord which held the cross around his neck and placed the cross in the palm of Lackmore's hand. Here," said John, "just in case you change your mind, my son. It belonged to my mother, so I hope that you wear it reverently, at least for her sake."

He then let go of Lackmore. When John let go of him, the palace guard took off like a shot, down the dark corridor and back- through the secret passageway which led to his bed chambers.

Lackmore was terrified that someone would see the incriminating tattoo on his chest, which denounced him as both a witch and a murderer. When he entered his room, he put on a new shirt, and he threw the old one on top of the dying embers of his fireplace. Lackmore watched the shirt as it went up in flames. Then he added another log to the dying fire.

"I'm in a sticky predicament," grumbled Lackmore. "It's all my fault for not killing you when I had a chance. What did you do to me, Oh, High Prince, and why did you spare me when you noticed my master's mark branded on my chest."

Karegan was first made aware of Lackmore's treachery when they were on a hunt together, and they got separated from the rest of their companions. The palace guard took off his woolen tunic because he got overheated, and Karegan could see straight through his friend's undershirt, which was drenched in sweat. Lackmore did not go through with his plans, though, and he told himself that it was all Karegan's fault.

The High Prince guessed that Lackmore was there to kill him, and instead of handing him over to the gallows, Karegan hid the mark by throwing his cloak over Lackmore's shoulders when the rest of their hunting party caught up with them. This was not a kindness that Lackmore deserved, and he knew it.

"What can I do now? I'm a dead man," groaned the palace guard to himself. "If I flee, the seven covens will only send someone else to do what I could not. Once you're taken care of, they will just hunt me down and kill me as well. No one says no to their coven and survives. And what about my poor sister? I'm all Ella has left since the death of our father."

Lackmore stood close to the fire. He didn't normally do that, but lately, he had started feeling unusually cold. And since it was the cold of the grave which the man felt, the fire did him no good. After his face went red and numb with the heat, Lackmore went back to the foot of his bed and sat down. The palace guard just sat there and stared at the poker in the corner of the room by the fireplace.

Now, if two men were to grapple with each other, the ordeal would usually resolve itself in a timely manner. But when a man wrestles with his own sense of decency, the struggle could take a lifetime to resolve itself. While Lackmore was grappling with his own conscience, Brother John headed back in the direction of the room where Gregor still lay sleeping. The little old priest felt cold, but it wasn't the chill of winter which made him suffer, and nor was it the cold of the grave like Lackmore felt. But rather, it was the cold of a indifferent world that afflicted the saintly old monk and made his heart ache like old bones in winter.

Brother John desperately wanted to see the kind face of a friend, however, the first person he bumped into when he left the dark and foreboding atmosphere of the King's dungeon was the cruel face of Victor. When he bumped into the old priest, Victor almost knocked him down, and he, much like Lackmore, turned and ran away. It was as if Brother John had suddenly contracted leprosy.

When John finally made it back to the room where Gregor still lay, he went straight to his bedside and collapsed on his knees. It was as though someone had placed the weight of the world on his shoulders, and he couldn't support the weight anymore while he was standing. As John knelt there, he began babbling again.

"Oh, foolish man, indifference makes you blind, and pride makes you deaf, so you can't see the mercy of heaven when it's offered to you, neither can you ask for it. What more could be done for you?" Gregor woke up when he heard John talking, and he asked, "What have I done, and how can I make amends for it, Father?"

"Oh, little one, you have done nothing wrong," said the old monk in a gentle voice. He then bent over Gregor and whispered something in his ear.

Karegan was lying on the floor near the fireplace, wrapped in his cloak, and next to him lay Dimitri and Malkovich. It was as if they expected someone to enter the room and threaten the life of the High Prince.

Karegan lay very still, but he was not asleep, though. But the only thing he could hear when Brother John started babbling were the names of Trestan and Lackmore. After John uttered these two names,

Gregor responded with an emphatic 'Yes.' After that, Brother John got up briefly to get a few things. Then he came back and gave the captain of the palace guards the last rights. When the saintly old priest had finished, Gregor turned over to his other side and fell asleep. When Gregor started snoring, Karegan got up and sat on a stool next to Brother John.

"So," said Karegan, "Gregor's a victim soul."

I am so glad Anetta isn't here to see him suffer, said John with a sigh. You're not going to be able to keep this from my sister, Said Karegan with a frown. Those two are twin souls, and the bond between Anetta and Gregor is even closer than the one that she has with me. My son, are you perhaps having trouble sleeping? Asked John. You shouldn't be worried about Gregor. The Divine Master has everything in his hands. When I laid down to rest, I saw the souls of those two assassins descend into eternal perdition, and it upset me so much that I couldn't sleep said the young Prince softly. An uncomfortable sort of silence fell upon the room after Karegan said this, and for a while, all that could be heard was the sound of Gregor, Dimitri, and Malkovich Snoring. The only people besides John who knew where the prisoners were being kept was the king of Duchaine and the palace guards. So, was there perhaps another palace guard besides Lackmore who belonged to a coven? It had to be, but who was it?

CHAPTER 12

Talk of War

he relative silence of the room was suddenly broken when there was a knock at the door. Dimitri got up and brushed himself off before he headed to see who it was. He approached the door cautiously, but he released his grip on his sword when he suddenly realized it was only Michellie.

Dimitri stepped outside of the room for a moment or so in order that he could speak to Michellie without disturbing anyone else inside the room.

"This had better be important," said Dimitri as he frowned at the palace guard.

"Your snoring keeps getting louder and louder as you age, old man," said Michellie with a grin. "I could hear you halfway down the hall."

Michellie often got his jollies from picking on the all too serious Dimitri, and it didn't help him any that embarrassment showed so easily on Dimitri's fair complexion.

The bodyguard glared at Michellie as he repeated, "What do you want?"

"Karegan is wanted by his father, and I've been sent to fetch him."

"Well, come on," said Dimitri as he opened the door and let the palace guard into the room.

It wasn't unlike Michellie to go out of his way just to annoy Dimitri when he was bored. And this was probably why the palace guard had such a mischievous twinkle in his eyes as he entered the room.

When Michellie entered the room, he approached Karegan and bowed deeply with one fist over his heart. As he did so, he said, "My most Sovereign Prince. You have been summoned by your Father to the great council hall."

Karegan tried getting up quickly, but Brother John stopped him by grabbing him by one shoulder.

"First, my son, you must fix your hair," said John as he produced a brush seemingly out of nowhere.

He then fussed with Karegan's hair as if he were his mother. Michellie made himself busy assisting Dimitri with his hair. But since there was nothing wrong with Dimitri's hair, the palace guard got his hand slapped by Dimitri. A little smile came to Karegan's lips as he watched Michellie tease his old bodyguard without mercy.

The High Prince got up after tying his hair back at the nape of his neck.

"I want you to stay here, Michellie until Brigitte and the others come. I want you to help them bring Gregor to his own room. Hopefully, he will be more comfortable there," said Karegan with a frown. "When you're done, I want you to meet me in the stables, but first, change into your warmest wool clothes. I'm going to hunt the sorcerer Doomlock, and I want you to get ready so that you can come with me."

Karegan then disappeared through the doorway and headed straight to the King's Great Council hall.

A sharp pain shot through his soul as he walked because he had once been friends with Doomlock. Both he and Doomlock were oracles of the Divine Master, but something happened to Doomlock. Some people believed that he was cursed by his father, Deathrogane, while others simply said that the young man fell into pride. But whatever the case be, Doomlock left the Santa De La Rosa and started a coven of his own.

Despite Doomlock's regrettable life choices, Karegan's heart bled for his old friend, and he deeply dreaded what he now had to do to stop him.

Dimitri called Karegan's name, and the High Prince suddenly realized that he had gotten so tied up in his own thoughts that he had stopped walking altogether and was standing in the middle of the hall with a far-off look on his face.

Karegan started walking once more in the direction of his father's council hall. But his mind was still on his old friend and the unfortunate measures, which he now had to take in order to stop him.

As Karegan walked, Dimitri and Malkovich followed close behind him. Although it was not intentional, the two bodyguards moved in unison. It was almost as if they were marching.

When Karegan entered the King's Great Council Hall, the site was a rather dramatic one. The tall doors were swung wide open by two palace guards in order to usher him into the room.

The council hall was grand, and the grandeur of the room rivaled that of the great banquet hall. In the center of the room was a long rectangular table. It had two long benches on either side of it for seats. In the center of the table, there were three large braziers to give light to the room. Both the head and the foot of the table was vacant today. Usually, King Ruben would have been sitting at the head of the table. But he was not doing so today because he wanted to establish an atmosphere of mutual respect between him and the old King of Merrick. This was despite the fact that he despised the man fiercely.

King Ruben sat at the right-hand side of the table with his Queen on one side of him. Karegan entered the room and sat on the other side of his father while Dimitri and Malkovich stood behind him.

Both men had a look of danger about them. Just on the other side of the table sat King Dinithall, and on either side of him sat one of his cronies. Both men were dressed in black, and while it wasn't easy to spot, Karegan knew that they both probably had an ominous mark on the palm of their hands.

It wasn't necessary to have Karegan present at the little meeting that day. However, King Ruben wanted the young Prince to have a taste of what it was like to do the job of a king.

The King of Duchaine whispered something in Karegan's ear, and he then stood up and said, "You have claimed that one of my father's servants hit one of your noblemen. That is a serious accusation and I would like to know what his name is so that I can address the issue promptly. Well, speak up, man."

Snapped Ruben as he remained seated despite the fact that everyone else was standing out of respect for the King of Merrick. "Her name is Brigitte," whispered King Dinithall, for he was terribly embarrassed to admit that one of his men had been roughed up by a woman.

King Ruben rubbed his chin as he desperately tried to contain his amusement over the situation. He made a hand gesture to one of the palace guards. The man left promptly to fetch the maidservant named Brigitte.

When he came back, he had her with him. Following shortly behind Brigitte was her whole entourage of younger maidservants.

"Brigitte, come here, girl," said King Ruben in a commanding voice as he stood up from his chair.

Brigitte obeyed him and stepped closer to the table.

"Did you hit one of King Dinithall's men?" asked Ruben.

"Yes, I did," admitted Brigitte in a frank tone of voice.

"But why?" asked Karegan with a frown.

The little old maidservant turned around without saying a word and made a hand gesture to one of the girls standing behind her.

There was a moment of confusion amongst her companions until she pointed out a girl about fifteen years of age and said come here, angel. The girl obeyed promptly and stepped closer to the older maidservant.

Brigitte pointed an accusing finger at King Dinithall and said, "His ruffians went around yesterday interrogating my girls. Just look what they did to poor Jewels."

Victor and Larson said that they were looking for a boy named Griffin. "Just look at what they did." As she spit out these last words of her sentence, She lifted the girl's chin and turned her face to one side so that the king of Duchaine could see her black eye.

"Oh, poor Jules," murmured King Ruben, who could no longer contain his amusement over the situation. Of course, he had always known that Brigitte was a force of nature, but watching the little woman take King Dinithall's thugs down a couple of notches was awesome, and it did his soul a great deal of good.

Karegan, who was just as amused as his father, asked, "So you hit him with a frying pan. Yes! And I told him that if he ever touched one of my girls again, I'd kill him!" Brigitte never had children of her own, but she was a natural-born mother. And King Ruben knew this.

"Good girl," said King Ruben. "From now on, we will call her terror of the witches."

King Ruben, at this point, was openly laughing over the situation. "That's all. You may go, woman." Said Karegan with a dismissive hand gesture.

When Brigitte was dismissed by the High Prince, she left quickly with her entourage of younger maids. King Ruben took a seat once again.

"Now that that's settled," said Karegan, who remained standing. "Was there anything else you wished to discuss?"

"Yes," said King Dinithall. "It appears that your father is preparing to go to war with Merrick. Our kingdoms have always been allies, so why are you building an army? If you feel threatened by our military force, remove your troops from our borders. Then we'll have a lasting peace."

"I, much like you, love peace. However, I love my freedom even more. And I'd rather die than surrender my country over to the hands of tyranny." King Dinithall went quiet and sat back down when Karegan said this. The old King had a stunned look on his face as he took his seat once again. He looked like someone had just punched him in the stomach. He was relieved at first when he learned that the High Prince was going to take part in the council that day. But by the time it was over the old King of Merrick wished that he was still just dealing with Ruben rather than his son. This is because the High Prince Karegan had the temperament of a young bull and he wouldn't give an inch on any of the subjects which were discussed.

Before the meeting was over, he had the audacity to demand that Brother John be released immediately. But that wasn't all. The young Prince also insisted that the man who was responsible for the death of Brother Lucas be brought to justice. Of course, King Dinithall played innocent. But everyone knew he was lying through his teeth when he claimed that Brother John was there on his own free will. The pious old monk would have never willingly violated his vow of stability.

When the meeting came to a close, everyone left the King's Great Council Hall except for King Ruben, the High Prince Karegan, and his two bodyguards.

"Goodbye, father," said the High Prince as he kissed King Ruben on the cheek.

"Where are you going, my son?" Asked King Ruben with a start.

"I'm going to hunt Doomlock and take his head. None of us are safe while he's alive," added the High Prince Karegan when he saw the doubt in his father's eyes. "I'm leaving Dimitri behind so that he can protect you. I know that he's loyal to a fault, and he will die before he lets anyone harm you or mother."

The look on his father's face when he said that was fraternal pride mixed with sadness. It is the look that crosses every father's face when he realizes that his son has become a man and is making difficult but mature decisions.

"Don't forget to say goodbye to your mother, boy. Oh, and you had better take Dimitri along with you. If he stays behind, I will have him hung for treason."

Karegan's face went seven shades of crimson when his father said this, but there was nothing that he could do but submit to his father's will. He left the room without saying anything else.

King Ruben stared intently at one of the braziers on the table as his son left the room.

Dimitri and Malkovich, for once, did not follow the High Prince Karegan. Instead, they lingered to say goodbye to their King.

"Farewell, my most sovereign Prince," said the two bodyguards as they bowed in unison.

They bowed so deeply, in fact, that one knee almost touched the floor.

King Ruben turned around, and to his great astonishment, the two men were actually speaking to him.

"Farewell, my dear friends, may the Divine Master grant you a long life and a peaceful death."

As he said this, King Ruben placed one fist over his heart and bowed deeply to the two men. This was a military salute used in Dimitri's homeland, and to receive such a greeting from a king was a tremendous honor.

After that, the two bodyguards turned and disappeared into the palace hall in pursuit of Karegan. Since the High Prince was walking briskly, it took a while for the two men to catch up with him.

Karegan went straight to his bed chambers and exchanged his exquisite clothes of a prince for those more suited for what he was about to undertake. After changing his clothes, he headed straight for the King's stables. But he was stopped by a man named Thornfield. The soldier was holding a jar of ointment.

"Here," said Thornfield as he handed the jar to Karegan. "Brother John seems to think that your friend has burned himself badly and is in need of this."

"Lackmore," whispered the High Prince under his breath as a little smile came to his lips.

Thornfield stared at him for a moment or so while he rubbed the black eye that Gregor had given him the day before. Then he turned and left, and Karegan turned around and headed in the direction of Lackmore's bed chambers.

An Unwanted Guest

ackmore stood directly in front of the hearth. He just stood there staring at a burning log as it slowly turned into coals. But after a while, he turned around, went back to his bed, and started changing into warm woolen clothes.

When he was all dressed, he pulled on his boots. After this, Lackmore reached for his sword and strapped it to his hip.

The man turned suddenly because he felt that someone was behind him.

"I hate it when I'm right," grumbled the palace guard under his breath as he found himself face-to-face with a man dressed all in black.

"How did you get in here, Larson?" asked Lackmore as he gripped the hilt of his sword tightly.

"The same as you," said Larson in a sing-song voice, which gave Lackmore the creeps.

"Well," said Lackmore, "I hope you have become acquainted with the King's Dungeon because there's a special place in there for men of your sort."

A faint smile came to Lackmore's lips as he said this.

"Are you threatening me, little bug?" asked Larson as he drew a cruel-looking dagger from its sheath.

Just as soon as his dagger cleared his sheath, Lackmore's sword was also drawn and ready to strike a death blow.

"Yes, I'm threatening you!"

"You degenerate Miss Crete!" growled Lackmore as a wild and dangerously angry look came to his eyes.

Lackmore hated Larson with a passion, and this was quite clearly shown by his attitude toward the man. The palace guard was very brawny, and he towered over Larson. Larson was terrified of him, and this was made evident by the fact that his hands began to shake when Lackmore drew his sword.

The palace guard only had to take one more step, and he would be close enough to take Larson's head clean off his shoulders with his sword.

Both blades gleamed in the dim light of the fireplace, which was the only light in the room. Both men were far too absorbed in their stare-down to notice the cold draft that was created when Victor entered the room through the secret passageway.

In fact, neither of them noticed Victor's presence until he snapped.

"Stop being foolish."

Larson and Lackmore obeyed and put away their weapons quickly.

Lackmore's face went white when he realized he was in the presence of Victor. This was probably because Victor was a shady sort of character, and no one who knew who he was would willingly let him enter their home. However, Lackmore was given very little say in the matter.

Victor wasn't nearly as tall as Lackmore, yet the palace guard had a sort of fearful respect for the man. This was probably because Victor was the person whom Doomlock usually sent when someone in the coven had stepped out of place.

He looked quite ordinary, though. If you didn't know any better, you might have thought Victor was harmless. But Lackmore knew better. Lackmore had a fearful respect for the man, and it was the same sort of respect that one would have for a sharp blade or a hot fire.

Larson, on the other hand, was a psychopath who enjoyed seeing people in pain, which is probably why Lackmore had such a disdain for him.

Of course, Lackmore was also a witch assassin. However, the palace guard had somehow managed to keep most of his humanity intact, while it was rather hard to believe that Larson even had a soul anymore.

There were still things Lackmore couldn't bring himself to do. He blamed his sister, Ella, for that fact because she deliberately kept reminding him that he had a soul that came from the hands of his Divine Master, and she stubbornly refused to give up on him.

But Lackmore secretly loved her for this, though.

"To what do I owe the pleasure of your company, Victor?" asked Larson, who was struggling to remain calm.

"Don't try smoothing things over with me, you traitor!" said Victor. "You were summoned to a secret meeting, and you didn't show up. Don't worry, we'll just have the meeting here today."

"He's a traitor. You said so yourself," said Larson as he pulled his dagger on Lackmore again.

Larson wasn't the sharpest person. And just as soon as he did so, Lackmore had his sword out once again.

Victor was about to say something brisk to the two men when a dark and mysterious figure entered the room.

The man's name was Rin, and he didn't start a coven of his own. He simply killed the head of another coven and took it over. He was known to be both ruthless and ambitious.

The man wore a deep hood over his head and a gray silk sash to hide his face. He always wore the finest gray wool money could buy, and it was said that no one had ever seen his face and lived to tell the tale.

Although his coven was relatively small, his name still struck terror in everyone who heard it.

For a moment, fear paralyzed the three men.

Victor and Larson seemed to mirror each other despite the fact that the two men had completely different appearances.

Victor had brown eyes and straight, shoulder-length hair, which was dyed black to hide his age.

Larson, on the other hand, had short, scraggly silver hair and a short, matching beard and mustache.

After observing the men before him, Rin said, "I've been sent by the council of the Seven Covens to clear up the mess which you fools have made. But I see that everyone isn't quite here yet. Oh well. I'm a patient man, and I can wait."

Perhaps Rin was telling the truth, and he had the patience of Job. However, everyone else in the room was desperate to get the whole thing over with.

After what seemed like an eternity, the tapestry that hung over the secret passageway moved once again as the King of Merrick arrived.

When Larson realized what was happening, he said, "I would like to present to you King Dinithall the Worthless, who killed his own wife and got beaten up by a girl with a sword in the King's Arena. Children will sing songs about him for a hundred years."

"It's not like you fared any better than he did in the Arena. I have always had the highest regard for Lady Anetta, but ever since I saw her throw you out of the King's Arena, I've been considering building a shrine in her honor."

"Not another word!" snapped Victor, who didn't appreciate being reminded of his humiliation in the King's Arena.

When King Dinithall entered the room, he had an unmistakable scowl on his face. This was probably because he had heard Larson mocking him as he entered the room.

"The Council of the Seven Most Powerful Covens has sent me here because the High Prince Karegan was supposed to have died almost a year ago. Yet the man is still very much alive. This presents a terrible problem for Doomlock and the Seven Covens.

"But Lackmore isn't the only person here who's standing in hot water."

"Why are we in trouble?" asked Larson, who didn't have the sense to keep his mouth shut.

"Victor and you were supposed to deliver Anetta to Lord Doomlock, and King Dinithall was supposed to make sure that happened. However, King Dinithall is a lustful pig, and Larson is a degenerate psychopath who enjoys seeing people suffer.

"Somehow, you three morons managed to let her go so that she could learn to use a weapon with great proficiency. Now, it will be quite difficult to get rid of her."

"Why not just let her go and focus on killing her brother?" asked Larson. "Anetta can't inherit the throne anyway because she's a woman. So I don't see why she's such a threat to the Seven Covens."

"True, she can't inherit the throne. However, she can still produce an heir to the throne if she marries a titled man. And the Witch Hunter Garic .." Rin paused in order to let Larson finish his sentence.

Of course, this was a trap.

"The Witch Hunter is a titled man," said Larson hesitantly.

"Bravo," said Rin as he clapped his hands. "You're not as stupid as I thought you were."

"We need to focus on what's in front of us," said Victor. "No one knows where Anetta is. She was taken away by the Witch Hunter. But the High Prince Karegan is right here, and he must die."

"I won't do it," said the palace guard resulootly.

Now, Lackmore truly hated Larson for being soulless.

However, there was only a fine line that separated the two men, and Lackmore knew this. The fact was, there were some things that Lackmore still couldn't bring himself to do.

Lackmore always knew, however, that there would come a day when his coven would tell him to do something unspeakable. On that day, he would have to choose between maintaining his sense of decency and becoming like Larson.

Finally, after years of sitting on the fence, that day had come.

"You have a beautiful sister," said Victor just as Lackmore reached for his woolen cloak which was draped over one side of the bed. "She is a pretty girl. Just a bit odd, but still beautiful! It would be a terrible shame if something bad were to happen to her."

Lackmore's blood ran cold when Victor mentioned his sister like that, but he wasn't about to just let the man bully him.

"Gentlemen," said Lackmore, who was trying to sound composed despite the fact that he was breaking out in a cold sweat. "I trust you know your way out, and I suggest you use it."

He then left his room and went sauntering down the hall in search of the High Prince Karegan. It didn't take long for the two men to bump into each other. In fact, they collided with each other so hard that Karegan almost dropped the jar of ointment that Brother John had sent for Lackmore.

"Here," said the High Prince as he handed the jar to his friend.

"What's this for?" asked the palace guard with a frown.

"Brother John wanted me to give it to you. He seems to think that you have burnt yourself or something."

Lackmore's face went red for a moment as he took the jar. He suddenly sensed that Karegan knew exactly what had happened.

After a moment of awkward silence, Lackmore said, "I was coming to look for you, and I am so glad I found you as quickly as I did. I must beg your leave of absence. I'm only asking three days' grace so that I can go home and see my family."

A look of alarm came to Karegan's face when Lackmore said this, and the palace guard tried to smooth things over by saying, "I'm homesick, and I wish to see my family."

Prince Karegan felt a surge of anger because he suddenly realized that Ella was in trouble because of Lackmore's stupidity.

Now, it was quite common for Karegan to give his friend a gentle pat on the back as a greeting. But when Karegan slapped the palace guard on the back this time, he was just a little rougher than he really intended to be.

Lackmore let out a pitiful sort of noise when Karegan did so.

"Take as much time as you need," said the High Prince. "I only ask that you take Drago with you, for I fear for your safety."

"Not Drago. Let me take Michellie instead."

When Lackmore noticed the perturbed look on his friend's face, he tried to smooth things over again by saying, "I hate Drago's guts, and I don't want to be stuck with his company for days on end."

"Very well," said Karegan. "Michellie will come with you."

The High Prince felt that Lackmore was hiding something from him, but he didn't press the matter any further. He just looked at his old friend intently for a moment before saying, "I am also headed for the stables myself, and I would very much enjoy your company if you would agree to walk with me there."

As they walked toward the stables, Karegan kept glancing at Lackmore with a sad little expression on his face. It was as though he wanted to say goodbye to his friend, but he just couldn't find the right words for his farewell.

Once they got to the stables, Lackmore went to saddle his horse, and Karegan took Michellie to one side under the pretext of saying goodbye to him.

To Karegan's great surprise, Michellie had trimmed his beard and hair, and he once again looked like himself.

When the two were out of earshot of the others, Karegan said, "There has been a change of plans. Lackmore has been playing with snakes, and now his sister Ella is in trouble because of him.

"He's defied his coven and removed his tattoo with a hot brand of some sort. I know that it doesn't rectify the wrongs that he has done. However, it is a step in the right direction."

"Lackmore is a timid man," said Michellie. "And it takes a lot of guts to do what he just did. You know they're going to hunt him down and kill him, don't you? Nobody says no to their coven and survives."

"I know," said Karegan. "I want you to go with him. I have every reason to believe that Victor will come to kill him. When he does, I want you to cut Victor's head off.

"His amnesty will expire the moment he leaves my father's palace. He's a murderer, and he's wanted all over Duchaine for his crimes."

"My Prince," said Michellie, "is it just my imagination, or are we both going on suicide missions?"

When he said this, Karegan became very sad, and he said, "What we are about to do is going to be exceedingly perilous. However, it is absolutely necessary that we do it."

Michellie tried to give the High Prince the same salute as before as he turned to leave, but Karegan stopped him by throwing his arms around the old palace guard's torso.

"Thank you, my Prince, for always treating me like an equal," said Michellie as Karegan squeezed him.

In fact, the High Prince squeezed him so tightly that the poor man could hardly breathe.

When Karegan let go of Michellie, the palace guard grabbed him by the shoulders and said, "Your Majesty, a Prince should never be seen weeping. Stay here for a moment till you compose yourself."

Karegan was, in fact, weeping profusely, like a frightened boy, and it took a moment or two for him to calm down.

Michellie, on the other hand, didn't even seem to be sad at all. He was as grave as a wise man, but he didn't feel sad. He merely felt cold.

The cold that Michellie felt was not the chill of winter, nor was it the cold of an indifferent world like Brother John suffered from. No, the cold that Michellie felt was the cold of the grave—much like Lackmore.

But Michellie had no reason to be sad about dying, for he was perfectly at peace with his conscience, and there wasn't anything left in this world that he was really all that attached to anyway. So the cold that he felt only left him feeling numb rather than melancholy, like Lackmore.

Michellie joined Lackmore. They mounted their horses and disappeared behind the horizon.

As soon as they had gone, Karegan, Dimitri, and Malkovich all departed as well.

CHAPTER 14

Into the Mountains

aric ran in a desperate attempt to catch up with Trestan. They ran frantically down the corridor of the secret passageway. It was as if all hell had broken loose and taken to chasing the boy.

Although Garic's age showed very little on his face, he could feel it in his bones as he struggled to keep up with Trestan.

When they finally came to a small door that led directly to the outside, Trestan had to stop for a moment so that Garic could catch his breath. When the old Deacon finally made it to where Trestan was, he was wheezing and struggling for breath. Just as soon as he caught his breath, Trestan took off again.

It wasn't long before Garic could smell the stables, and this brought a smile to his lips. When they arrived at the stables, they quickly found that Garic's mare was saddled and ready to ride. Beside Garic's mare were two black geldings. The two geldings were from the King's own stock, and Garic could tell straight away that they were eastern-bred horses.

"The old King knows what I like to see in a horse," whispered Garic as he tied his sack full of Anetta to one of the gelding's saddles.

"Can you ride, child?" asked Garic as he handed the reins of his silver mare to Trestan.

"Just a little bit," said the boy as he mounted the horse.

As he did so, the spirit wolves let out another eerie howl, and Garic said,

"You had better pick it up quickly and ride like your life
depends upon it because tonight, it really does."

After saying this, the old witch hunter mounted his horse and took off like a shot, and Trestan followed shortly behind him.

For a short period of time, they were followed by another rider dressed in gray, but they eventually lost him because Garic took a trail through the Daroogian forest, which was rarely used. Garic had planned on reaching the mountains by dawn.

However, Trestan kept getting thrown from Garic's mare, which slowed their travel down considerably.

At about noon, the old witch hunter decided to make camp because the horses were tired, and Trestan couldn't go any further without rest and a bite to eat.

As the two men sat under a grove of evergreens, the sack began to twitch and make noise.

"In my experience, girls are often like any other fierce little critter, and it's always best to get these things over with quickly," said Trestan with a frown. "But when you let her go, I would like to stand at a safe distance so that she doesn't try to tear my face off or stab me with one of her daggers."

So Garic agreed to this arrangement, and he let Trestan stand at a safe distance when he went to let Anetta out of the sack.

As Garic approached the sack, a stream of muffled threats and profanity issued forth from it. He quickly untied the top of the sack and dumped its contents on the ground at his feet.

After letting Anetta go, the old Deacon took three steps backward because he didn't want to be stabbed.

"Wow, your majesty! I would never have guessed that you had such a broad and diverse vocabulary," said Garic with a broad smile.

Anetta had been in the burlap sack for quite some time, and she blinked for a moment because the sunlight hurt her eyes. When she realized that Garic was standing over her, she went for her dagger. When she remembered that she no longer had it, she frowned. Brother John had made her hand it over to Lord Rosalyn the night before.

Anetta stood up, and Garic took a few more steps backward in order to put a safe distance between him and Anetta. It was remarkable, though, that the man didn't trip because the ground that he was standing on was so uneven.

"Garic, take me back home, or I'll have your head on a pike!"

"Girly, I owe faulty to your father, and he has ordered me to take you to a convent in the mountains. Because I'm a man of honor, I intend to do so."

"No! I'm not going with you! You had better take me home at once!"

"So, despite the fact that the Seven Covens are hunting you, you still want to go home?"

"Yes!" growled Anetta.

"OK," said Garic as he went to untie the two geldings.

Once he untied them, he offered the reins of one of the horses to Anetta.

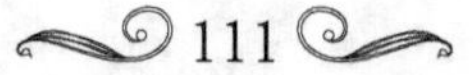

After taking a moment to fix her hair, she snatched the reins from his hands. She then mounted the gelding and took off in a random direction.

Garic smiled mischievously as he watched Anetta disappear into the forest, for it was highly unlikely that she would be able to find her way back home from where she was. This was because the old Deacon had taken an obscure path through the woods, and few souls were even aware that it existed.

The fact that Anetta had ridden all night in a flour sack would have made it impossible, even for a person with the most innate sense of direction, to find their way back home again.

Trestan joined Garic as Anetta disappeared into the woods, and he asked in disbelief, "You let her go?"

"Oh, she'll be back," said Garic with a little chuckle as he crossed his arms over his chest. He was obviously very pleased with himself. And sure enough, Anetta did indeed come back.

However, she was far too proud to admit her defeat that easily. So, Anetta just turned the horse around and headed in a different direction. She did this several times until she finally admitted to herself that she was hopelessly lost.

She dismounted the horse in order to ask Garic for directions. This was terribly humiliating for her, though.

Garic was sitting under a giant cedar tree, eating apples and laughing about something Trestan had said when he was approached by Anetta. She looked very much like a wet cat when she stepped close to the old Deacon.

"How do I get back to my father's palace?" asked Anetta, who looked absolutely frazzled.

Garic, who had his mouth full of apple and didn't even take the time to chew and swallow before answering, said,

"I said that you could leave if you wanted to. However,
I never promised to give you directions."

Anetta threw a rock at his head when he said this, but luckily, she wasn't all that serious about hitting him, so she missed.

Anetta knew that it was no use arguing with Garic anymore, so she sat on the ground with her back against a boulder and fell asleep.

When she awoke, the day was mostly spent, and there was a small pile of rocks beside her. Garic approached her when she woke up and said,

"I made sure that your Majesty had plenty of rocks for
target practice so you don't miss next time."

Just as soon as he said this, though, Anetta picked up a pebble and flung it at Garic's head. This time, she hit her mark perfectly.

Garic gave her a dirty look as he handed her a bow and a quiver full of arrows.

"I saw a clearing not too far from here where wild rose bushes grow. You can't miss it. I would like you to go there and get us a rabbit for supper."

Now, Garic really didn't expect Anetta to come back with a rabbit. In fact, he didn't even think she knew how to use a bow at all. He merely wanted a pretext to get rid of her while he dressed the wounds on Trestan's back. This was because he knew it would upset Anetta if she saw them.

Once she was gone, Garic quickly cleaned and dressed the wounds on the boy's back. Once they were covered up again, the old Deacon breathed a sigh of relief because seeing the wounds caused him a great deal of distress.

Anetta certainly was not hunting for rabbits, though. Rather, she had gone looking for a road so that she could find her way back home again. It wasn't long before she found what she was looking for.

As the sun went down, the cold air became unbearable for her because she was still wearing the silk dress from the night before. She had no cloak to keep her warm either, and the cold north wind cut straight through her.

To make matters even worse, it started snowing. But luckily, an old peddler who was riding his horse and cart to a nearby town saw her and took pity on her. He offered her a ride.

When she refused his offer, the old peddler countered her by saying, "Brother John would be cross with me if he learned that I let a child such as yourself freeze out here in the cold."

After a moment or so of considering the old man's offer, she finally accepted it, but only because she saw the cross around his neck, which was affiliated with Brother John's order.

Anetta highly doubted that the man was lying to her when he claimed to know Brother John, and she got into the back of his cart. He covered her with a heavy wool blanket and took her to town.

The blanket wasn't very clean, but it was so cold that Anetta really didn't care that much, for at least she was warm. When they entered the town, the old peddler left Anetta near the inn.

Anetta had no money, so she went in search of stables where she could stay the night. The air was so cold that Anetta could see her own breath. As she walked, Anetta tried desperately to warm her hands by tucking them under her arms because they had gone numb with the cold.

A man came out of nowhere, though, and he grabbed her, put her in an arm lock, and dragged her into a nearby tavern against her will.

"My lady, you are exceedingly imprudent for traveling alone," said the stranger as he threw his cloak around Anetta. He did so in such a way that it completely enveloped her so he could hide her identity.

"Don't struggle, woman, or I'll break your arm, so help me!" said the stranger as he led her to a table in the darkest corner of the tavern, after which he seated himself on the other side of it.

"Don't move a muscle, and keep your head down. There have been several men following you, Princess. They were all dressed in black, and it's my guess they've been sent to kill you."

"How do you know who I am?" asked Anetta as she rubbed her hands together nervously and wished she had a dagger.

"Everyone knows who you are, Princess Anetta," said the man as he produced a dagger and slid it across the table to her.

"Here," said the stranger, "I've been told that you're good with knives."

Anetta took the dagger, and her face went white because she realized it was the very same one that she had given to Lord Rosalyn the night before.

"Where did you get this?" asked Anetta, who was filled with alarm.

"A friend gave it to me," said the man as he lit a pipe and began to smoke. Anetta observed the man in front of her nervously.

He had dark eyes and black hair, which almost reached his shoulders. His hair was held back from his face by a gray scarf.

He was a little younger than she was, and his facial features were vaguely familiar to her. His wispy black facial hair, which was little more than peach fuzz, was cut back into a goatee. His nose was slightly alkaline. His skin had an olive hue to it, and the stranger's appearance reminded Anetta of a gypsy or a wild man of sorts.

Anetta felt like she knew him somehow.

"Garic," murmured Anetta under her breath.

"I beg your pardon?" said the stranger as he pulled the pipe from between his lips for a moment to frown at her.

"You look like Garic."

Just as soon as those words left Anetta's mouth, she felt a terrible stab of regret, for she really didn't know who this strange man was. What if he was up to no good?

"I think I have the right to look like Garic if I want to," said the man. "After all, he is my father."

When he said this, Anetta's eyes narrowed.

"You are either a fool or a liar. Everyone knows that Garic never had any children," said Anetta angrily.

She added, "He's a consecrated man. How dare you insinuate such a thing about him?"

Anetta blinked because she suddenly realized that she was defending the man who had literally drugged her with Rot Root tea and kidnapped her. It baffled her that she actually cared that much about the old Deacon's reputation, but she really did care.

"Garic was once married before he became a Deacon. His wife's name was Lady Catalina, and Lady Catalina was my mother. So that would make Garic my father."

"The only way you can argue with me, my lady, is to impute my mother's honor."

"Lady Catalina died before she had any children," protested Anetta.

"My mother was just a week shy of her due date when she died. The man who killed her was a surgeon, and he cut me out of her womb to save my life. That very same man raised me.

"He tried very hard to raise me in the occult, but it didn't work for either of us, and I ran away from home. I lived in the Wilds until I met Lord Rosalyn. I've been working for Lord Rosalyn as his spy."

The stranger sighed deeply because the incredulous look on Anetta's face just wouldn't go away.

"I have no way of proving what I say to you, my lady," said the stranger. "And you obviously have trust issues."

Anetta's face went red with embarrassment because she realized that she was gripping the hilt of her dagger tightly.

Just then, a woman came with a tray of food.

"I added an extra cup of mulled wine and a bowl of soup for your young friend here, and don't even think of paying me back," said the old woman.

Her name was Helen. She was a kind-faced, elderly woman. She was heavyset, and all of her hair was silver.

"Thank you, Helen," said the stranger with a warm smile.

"Now you'd better hurry up and eat, then make yourself scarce, my son. Two men wearing black came in here earlier today, and they were inquiring about you."

After saying this, the woman left the table, and the stranger began inhaling his soup as if he was starving.

The man suddenly stopped eating, though, and dropped his spoon when he saw Anetta crossing herself so that she could say grace. The stranger also blessed himself and said grace very quickly, as if he was afraid someone would take his food away from him and he would starve.

Just as soon as he finished, he picked up his spoon once more and continued eating like a heathen.

Anetta had barely started eating by the time the stranger had finished his bowl of soup.

"Do you want any of the bread?" asked the man in a muffled voice.

Anetta looked up from her soup, and she noticed that most of the bread was gone.

"You had better eat it, seeing that you're so hungry."

Anetta tried to eat her soup as quickly as possible because she was afraid that the stranger would decide to inhale her food as well.

"I'm sorry I didn't introduce myself to you before, my lady," said the man. "My Christian name is Sarius, but most people just call me Rin."

The man's voice was muffled because his mouth was stuffed with bread.

"Nice to meet you, Rin," said Anetta. "You already know my Christian name. My father calls me child, and my friends call me girly, but if you try using either of those names on me, I will cut you. I promise."

"Yes, Your Majesty," said Rin, as he chuckled softly in spite of the fact that his mouth was still stuffed full of bread.

His mirth was short-lived, however, because he suddenly noticed that the music had stopped and everyone was leaving the room. In fact, the only people left in that room aside from him and Anetta were four assassins, all dressed in black.

Both Anetta and Rin stood up almost at the same time. When they did so, they were rushed by the four assassins.

Rin drew two swords from their sheaths and slid one across the table to Anetta just before ducking to avoid getting his throat slashed by a man with a poisoned dagger. He then quickly ended the man with a death blow from his sword.

He also took care of two of the other men as well.

This only left one man for Anetta to deal with. But the man that Anetta got stuck with just happened to be a tall, burly man with strong arms, and he tried to crush her with the table.

After grappling with the assassin for a bit, Anetta threw herself to the floor on her back, slid between the man's ankles, then flung Rin's sword into the back of his head.

The sword killed the man very quickly, and he fell forward with a crash, smashing one of the tables on his way to the floor.

Someone notified the local magistrate, and they arrived to apprehend the villains who were destroying poor Helen's tavern.

When the men arrived, Rin escaped through the back door, leaving Anetta to take the blame for the wreckage and devastation that was left after the scuffle with the four assassins.

CHAPTER 15

Rattigan's Dungeon

everal tables and chairs had been smashed. The front door was torn off its hinges, and there was even a small fire in the corner that started when a lantern had been overturned during the scuffle.

The fire was quickly put out, and it caused very little damage to the place. The only person left standing in the room when the authorities arrived was Anetta. This was because Rin had made himself scarce so that he wouldn't be caught by them.

The magistrate apprehended Anetta for questioning. However, since she refused to cooperate with him, he simply had her thrown into Lord Rattigan's dungeon.

When Anetta set foot in the dungeon, she looked much like a queen walking into her court. So dignified was her carriage, and this made Lord Rattigan wonder who on earth the girl actually was.

Anetta didn't get much sleep that night, but neither did Garic, who went to find her.

He followed her tracks to the road. It didn't take long for Garic to figure out where Anetta was once he arrived at the tavern. The old Deacon went to see Anetta right away after visiting Lord Rattigan for a few days.

In fact, Garic had actually planned on letting Anetta stay in the dungeon for a whole week or so just to teach her a lesson because of all the trouble she had caused him.

She started coughing after a few days in the cold, damp dungeon, and so Garic went to get her out because he became concerned about her health. But he made her swear to him that she would never again leave him without first getting his permission. She also had to tell him where she was going and when she would be back.

In short, Garic was treating Anetta very much like a child, and she didn't appreciate this at all.

Garic wrote the oath on a piece of parchment and handed it to Anetta through the bars of her cell.

She just stood there for a moment and glared at the old Deacon before taking the piece of parchment and reading the oath out loud. As she did, she held one hand over her heart.

Anetta added a little clause of her own just because she could. She said at the very end, "May the Almighty God hold me bound to this oath until Garic shall release me, or Father Ivan grant me an exemption from it."

"There," said Anetta. "Are you happy now?"

"No!" said Garic. "But since you're set on being a mule, I guess I'll just have to take what I can get.

"Besides, I doubt we'll meet up with Father Ivan anytime soon, so it's not a big deal anyway."

Garic said this because Father Ivan was just the sort of person who would actually agree to give Anetta an exemption from her oath. Anetta didn't know this, but Garic did.

He let Anetta out of the cell, and she enjoyed a nice hot bath followed by a hot, homemade meal.

In fact, she had dinner with Lord Rattigan and his wife.

The next morning, Anetta sent for Garic so that she could speak to him in private.

"So you have finally decided to apologize to me for your horrible behavior," said Garic with a little smile.

"No! I will never apologize to you!" said Anetta.

Garic suddenly felt the urge to laugh. It was the same sort of urge that a parent gets when their small child says something cute but naughty.

Garic somehow managed to remain completely stoic, however.

Anetta thought he was actually being cross with her, though, but in reality, he really was trying his hardest not to laugh.

"I called you here because I met your son the other day," said Anetta. "He saved my life. If it weren't for him, I'd probably have died in poor Helen's tavern."

"I'm a Deacon, girly. Exactly what are you suggesting?"

Anetta blinked for a moment as she realized that what she said had come out all wrong.

What she meant to say was, "I met a man who claimed to be your son." However, she was so excited by the idea of Garic actually having a son that what she said came out wrong.

"I'm suggesting that your wife somehow gave birth before she died."

Anetta winced the instant these words left her mouth because they also came out terribly wrong as well.

"That simply just can't be true!" said Garic as he ran his fingers through his curly black hair in an effort to contain his distress.

He was obviously still grief-stricken over the loss of his wife.

Anetta thought that he was calling her a liar, though. Since her nerves were already frazzled, it just took one little thing to push her over the edge.

Her thinking that the old Deacon was calling her a liar was the last straw for her.

Garic became terribly uncomfortable when Anetta started crying, and his discomfort was so great he momentarily forgot about his own grief, which he felt so acutely.

Garic had spent the last fifteen years since the death of his wife adopting random spiritual children.

In fact, the High Prince of Merrick actually called the old witch hunter Father. And so did many other young men at the Santa Dè La Rosa.

But never before had Garic been sent to look after a girl. And he found himself way out of his comfort zone when Anetta started weeping.

As he watched her start to cry, a look of worry came to his face, and he recalled something that Brother Lucas used to say about women.

The old monk used to say, "If you send me against a woman weeping, I will quickly be defeated."

Brother Lucas had been married for thirty years before his wife died, and he became a monk. As a result, he had much wisdom where women were concerned.

Garic cautiously pulled a stool up next to the bed and sat on it so that he could talk to the princess face to face. But she had a pillow pressed against her face because she was embarrassed by the fact that she was crying in front of Garic.

He tried to pull the pillow away first before speaking to her. But even his best efforts were of no use because she had a death grip on it. So Garic decided to work around the pillow.

"I'm sorry, child," said the old Deacon in a gentle voice.

Anetta instantly dropped the pillow from her face when Garic called her this, and she growled.

"I'm not a child, Garic! I'm an adult! Don't you dare treat me like a child! That's just demeaning!"

"I'm sorry I upset you, girly," said Garic as he finally managed to wrestle the pillow away from her hands.

"Would you please tell me what I have done wrong so that I can make peace with you, child?"

At that moment, Garic suddenly reminded Anetta of his brother Gregor because, while Garic was most certainly a barbarian, he wasn't without honor. Despite his rough manners, Anetta actually felt safe in his presence.

After considering the old Deacon for a bit, Anetta ripped the pillow away from his hands and hit him in the face with it.

"There, that's for calling me a liar," said Anetta.

She then hit him a second time with the pillow and said, "That's for insinuating that I'm childish. Now that we have rectified the wrongs you have done, you may go so that I can make myself ready. Lord Rattigan's wife has invited me to breakfast, and I'm starving."

"My lady," said Garic, "you must get ready to leave at once if you wish to make good time. Otherwise, we'll be forced to make camp in the woods several times before we get to the convent. And since it's the dead of winter, you'll not be very happy if we get stuck in a blizzard."

"I have already told you I'm not going!" said Anetta defiantly.

"You are coming with me, girly, either riding in a saddle or stuffed in a sack. It's your decision."

Garic barely avoided getting hit by one of Anetta's shoes as he ducked out the door.

Anetta glared at the door for a moment or so after the old Deacon left. She then quickly got ready for a ride into the mountains because she knew all too well that Garic was in earnest, and if she didn't do as she was told, the old Deacon would stuff her back into that sack, which smelled like a goat.

Garic laughed to himself as he left Anetta's room. The princess was nineteen, yet she still managed to have the personality of a very small child, and the old Deacon found it quite amusing to pick on her.

When Anetta entered Lord Rattigan's stable, she was wearing a dark blue woolen dress and a matching hooded cape lined with the pelts of sheep.

Trestan had also changed his clothes. In fact, he and Garic were both dressed in the same fashion. That is, they were both wearing plain gray woolen trousers with matching tunics and capes. In short, they were dressed quite plainly.

Anetta had never before seen Trestan without his monk's habit. At first glance, she mistook him for a child. This was quite easy to do, considering how stunted his growth was.

Anetta asked him, "Where's your mother, boy?"

"I have no mother, my lady," admitted Trestan sadly.

"Oh, I'll be your mother!" exclaimed Anetta. "Can I pinch your cheeks?"

Trestan's face turned red at the prospect of getting his cheeks pinched by Anetta, and he was saved right in the nick of time by Garic, who shouted, "Don't touch him, child! He's been playing with snakes. He could be rabid."

When Garic said this, Anetta recoiled her hand as if Trestan had suddenly become leprous.

Trestan held out the palm of his hand in order to show Anetta his tattoo.

"I'm not a child, my lady," said Trestan in a hoarse voice. "I'm a witch and a murderer. I sold my soul, and I'm dangerous, so you had better stay clear of me."

He then added in a whisper, "However, I would love to have a mother."

After a moment or so of awkward silence, Garic mounted his horse, and Anetta and Trestan followed suit. As soon as the three of them left the stables, they were met by Lord Rattigan, who was also on horseback.

"The people of the town wish to say goodbye to Anetta," said Rattigan. "You see, she has sort of become a local hero after she dispatched those four assassins the other night, and they wish to thank her." Garic agreed to the little arrangement.

Once Lord Rattigan got the okay from Garic, he rode his horse ahead to inform the townspeople that Anetta was planning on passing through their town.

Just as soon as Rattigan was gone, Anetta pulled her horse next to Garic's and explained to him for a second time that she was helped by a man who looked like him.

"He said his name was Rin," said Anetta.

Garic's blood ran cold when Anetta mentioned that name, and before she could say any more, he interrupted her.

"Did you say his name was Rin?"

As Garic spoke, a look of consternation crossed his face.

"Yes. Why does that matter?" asked Anetta with a frown.

"I've been hunting a man named Rin for nearly a year, and he's always managed to elude me," said Garic. "It's said that nobody's ever seen his face and lived to tell the tale.

"You are very lucky, girly if you really met Rin and you saw his face."

"If that's true, then why did he help me? Why did he kill the other assassins to save my life?" asked Anetta.

"It's not unusual for there to be squabbles amongst the covens."

Just then, they began entering the town, and as they rode through the square, the people gathered and cheered for Anetta.

Garic dismounted and led his horse with one hand and Anetta's with the other. He kept looking for assassins dressed in black hiding amongst the crowd. However, he was not looking out for a man dressed all in gray wool, so he completely missed Rin, who blended in well with the local people.

"I'm no hero," grumbled Anetta under her breath.

"They believe you are, so just play along," growled Garic almost in a whisper.

The townspeople lined up on either side of the square, and when they saw Anetta, they cheered for her loudly.

Silence broke out, though, when the woman who owned the tavern stepped out of the crowd and approached Anetta. The woman was carrying a sword, and she insisted on giving the weapon to Anetta herself.

No matter how much Garic protested, the old woman still held her ground. So finally, after contending with the old woman for several minutes, Garic gave in and let her pass so that she could give Anetta the sword herself.

When the kind old woman handed her the weapon, Anetta tried to refuse it at first, stating firmly that it wasn't hers, but the old woman insisted that it was a gift from Rin.

This made the hair on Garic's back stand on end.

It didn't help any when the old woman added, "He's keeping an eye on you, my lady, to ensure that you leave here safely."

Garic was already uneasy enough as it was, and he started scanning the crowd in search of the man called Rin.

As he did so, he felt a deep stab of regret, for it was very likely that he had carelessly put Anetta's life in jeopardy by parading her through the streets like a hero.

Garic didn't see Rin amongst the crowd of people.

Anetta thought that she saw him, however. She wasn't sure at first because his face was covered with a silvery-gray scarf. But as she rode through the square, the man got closer to her.

When he made eye contact with her, he gave her a little wink and then disappeared into the crowd again.

Garic was so busy looking for Rin that he had completely missed him altogether.

The rest of the journey out of town proved rather uneventful, and Garic was glad of it, for no one loves boredom like a bodyguard does.

As nightfall came, Garic and his companions were about to stop and make camp when they heard spirit wolves once more.

A wild chase then ensued.

Every time they slowed down or stopped, it wasn't long before the spirit wolves caught up with them once more.

Finally, at the end of the second day, the horses could go no further. And even if they were fresh, they would not have been able to outrun the werewolves because they had been completely surrounded by them this time.

As the sun set on the second day, they all rode their horses into a small clearing that lay between the Daroogian forest and the great mountains.

All three of them dismounted and stood in a huddle in the center of the clearing.

"What will happen once they catch us?" asked Anetta nervously.

"They will tear us to pieces," said Trestan, who was terrified.

He kept looking around himself with eyes as big as saucers, for he was scared out of his wits because he had once seen firsthand what spirit wolves could do when they caught their prey.

Trestan began to sing in an effort to remain calm.

The shadow wolves could be seen moving through the trees of the forest, but unlike real wolves, they were vaguely transparent, like dark gray smoke, and they had glowing red eyes.

As they grew closer and closer, Garic drew his sword.

"Will that help?" asked Anetta.

"No, but it makes me feel better to think that I can die with my boots on," said Garic.

The shadow creatures grew closer and closer, and when everyone was sure that this was the end, a bright golden burst of light broke out at the edge of the forest.

CHAPTER 16

Waiting for help

ather Ivan, who was the pious Abbot of the Santa Della Rosa, went in pursuit of Brother John's captors when he was abducted. But Ivan was so sick that he was eventually forced to wait in a cave until help came.

He wasn't alone, though, because a wolf named Lobos kept him company.

The ginormous wolfdog was Anetta's pet, but he had taken a peculiar shine to the old Abbot, and he often brought Ivan things he had stolen. Most of the items were from various little villages, but it surprised the old priest when Lobos brought him a bag containing vestments, a clean habit, and a few other things needed to perform his priestly functions.

The habit was especially welcomed by the old priest, but to his great dismay, it was far too short on his legs and too tight around the arms as well.

But since Father Ivan's old habit was soiled by bloody vomit, he was greatly relieved to have something clean to wear, and he thanked his Divine Master heartily.

The old Abbot laughed a little to himself when he ripped both sleeves almost completely off his habit as he reached above his head to consecrate the Eucharist during Mass. For the first time in a very long time that night, Father Ivan actually felt hungry. After cleaning a rabbit that Lobos had caught for him, he roasted it over his little campfire.

He didn't eat much, though on account of the gnawing pain in the pit of his stomach, and the ginormous wolfdog was eager to finish Ivan's supper for him.

After saying his prayers the best he could by memory, Father Ivan thanked Lobos for supper by giving him a thorough belly rub. After that, the old Abbot turned in for the night.

Ivan fell asleep quickly, and he started to dream.

He dreamt that there was a man standing in a clearing, calling out to him for help.

The old priest woke up with a start. He went straight to the bag of things that Lobos had brought him, said a little prayer, and then took the first things that he picked up out of the cave and into the bleak darkness of that dreary winter night.

The instant that the spirit wolves melted away, Garic knew beyond a shadow of a doubt that he was in the presence of his Divine Master.

It was as if the pious old Deacon heard a call that no one else heard, and he went running off into the darkness.

Garic found Father Ivan just before he fainted, and the old Deacon was just in time to prevent the small reliquary that held the Blessed Sacrament from falling on the ground.

When Father Ivan came to, he was in his cave once more. His old campfire was blazing in a lively fashion, and Anetta was sitting on the other side of it, weeping on account of a dream she had about Gregor.

When Anetta realized that Father Ivan was awake, she brought him a cup of tea to bring his temperature down.

It had a vile aftertaste, and Ivan had to force himself to drink it after the first sip.

The Lady Anetta knew her herbs, though, and the tea worked wonders once the old priest managed to finish it.

Anetta went back to her place by the fire and sat down after giving Ivan his tea. She had not slept well for nearly a week on account of a dream she kept having.

It was always the same thing, though.

She dreamt that she was standing in front of a table. Lackmore was seated at the head of the table, Trestan was seated at the foot of it. Each man had a cup in front of him, and into these cups, a mysterious figure poured each man's misdeeds and transgressions.

When this strange figure left the room, the contents of both cups turned into monsters, and they threatened to devour the two men at the table.

However, Gregor came in with a cup of his own, emptied the other two cups into his, and drank it all almost in one swallow.

When he did this, the two monsters disappeared into thin air.

Trestan and Lackmore left the room. Lackmore entered a garden full of flowers and fruit, while Trestan chose a painful path full of thorns and suffering, which led directly to the Santa Dalo Rosa.

Once he got there, the monks declared him their Abbot.

Gregor remained standing in the room, and he looked like he had ingested poison. He turned towards Anetta and asked, "Will you also leave me? Am I perhaps to suffer this alone?"

Anetta had this dream several times, and she always awoke from it crying.

She wore her hood down to hide the fact that she was weeping from her companions, but Father Ivan noticed right away when she brought him tea.

Anetta wanted desperately to join Garic in adoration of the Divine Master, but the old Deacon was so engrossed in prayer that she didn't think it right to intrude on him.

So, Princess Anetta sat by the fire, sharpening the sword that Rin had given her. But since the man kept the weapon as sharp as possible, she was actually dulling it.

After a few moments of prayerful thought, Father Ivan went over to Anetta and sat down.

"May I?" asked Father Ivan as he reached for her sword.

After a moment or so of hesitation, she passed her weapon to him.

Father Ivan gave the weapon a good look over. It wasn't a traditional cross-hilt sword of a knight. Rather, it resembled a wakizashi, and the old priest could tell right away that it was a custom-built weapon for a rogue assassin.

Father Ivan got up to do forms, which was probably a mistake because he was rather dizzy, but somehow, he made it through with very little trouble.

Father Ivan had a kind and gentle demeanor despite the scar on his right cheek, and the sword looked odd in his hands. However, when he stood up and started doing forms, he was poetry in motion, and it was as if he was born with a sword in his hands.

He was once a famous knight of Relic, and when he started doing forms with the sword, Anetta could have easily believed it.

When Ivan brought the weapon back, he had broken out in a sweat.

"Here, my lady. It's a beautiful weapon. Does Your Majesty perhaps have a secret admirer?"

"No!" said Anetta emphatically. "He was more like a guardian angel, and he saved my life when I was attacked by assassins.

"He claimed to be Garic's son. Well, is it possible, Father? Could the stranger have been telling me the truth?"

"Well, this man probably does believe that he is Garic's son, and perhaps the two men bear some sort of resemblance to each other, but that doesn't mean anything.

"It is quite possible that someone lied to your young benefactor about his parents."

"Are you saying that it is impossible for his story to be true?"

"Nothing is impossible, my dear. This man's story, however, is so incredible that it's rather hard to swallow.

"But if he has claimed Garic as a father, what of it? Many young men at the Santa Dalo Rosa called Garic 'Father' as boys.

"I believe that it has done them a great deal of good because young men tend to emulate their father figure."

"Speaking of Garic, where on earth is he?" asked Father Ivan with a frown.

"He's in adoration," said Anetta with a shrug.

"For how long?" asked the old priest.

"Two days," said Anetta. "Why?"

"I'll be back in a moment," said the old Abbot as he got up.

Ivan went over to where the reliquary, which held the Blessed Sacrament, was, and he consumed the host. Then he sent Garic to lay down near the fire.

Before returning to his place next to Anetta, though, the old Abbot covered Trestan with a blanket from one of the saddlebags.

Trestan lay tied up in a corner of the cave because he had gone crazy in front of the Blessed Sacrament.

"Father, perhaps if you saw him, you would also believe the young man's story, too," said Anetta firmly.

"He looked like Garic, talked like him, smelled like him. Why, they even have the same table manners," said Anetta.

Garic, who was just on the other side of the fire, heard what Anetta said because he wasn't asleep, and he groaned.

"For the last time, woman, I don't have any children!"

After that, Garic got up to join the conversation because he found it impossible to sleep when Father Ivan and Anetta were talking about him.

"Well, my lady," said Father Ivan in an attempt to change the subject. "However, did you manage to get all the way out here with this guy?"

"Well," said Anetta. "He drugged me with Rot-root tea and stuffed me in a bag."

Garic looked horribly innocent when Anetta said this, and he tried to dodge when Father Ivan, who was sitting next to Garic, reached over and grabbed the old witch hunter by the ear.

"Ow, ow, ow, ow, ow," said Garic, though it obviously didn't hurt him that much.

Finally, when Father Ivan let go of Garic's ear, he smacked him on the back of the head.

"I thought I told you never to do that again, boy!" said the old Abbot sternly.

"It's not my fault she drank the wrong tea," protested Garic in his own defense.

"You're lucky she only gave you a black eye. As I recall, Lady Catalina tried to kill you when you did that to her."

"Oh," said Anetta. "I gave him the black eye when he made me dance with him. I really didn't mean to, though. He just didn't duck quickly enough."

Father Ivan took a moment to frown at Garic. Then he turned to Anetta and said, "You must excuse this barbarian, my lady. He was raised by heathens in the mountains, and he barely knew his mother."

This little comment from the old Abbot left Anetta in stitches because she knew full well that Father Ivan and Brother John were the heathens who raised Garic and Gregor.

"My dear," said Father Ivan. "Go and get me some firewood, would you, my lady? My bones are old, and the cold makes them ache."

The fire was, in fact, dying. However, Anetta doubted that was why she was being sent out of the cave, and she was right.

When she left, the Abbot turned to Garic and said, "What do you plan on doing with the boy? He can't stay with you! He's a threat to the princess.

"He's dangerous, Garic."

Just when Garic was about to answer Ivan, Anetta came rushing back.

Once she caught her breath, she announced, "There are several people coming on donkeys, and they appear to be monks."

Shortly after this, they were joined by several monks from Father Ivan's order.

At first, Father Ivan was cross with them because he thought they had disobeyed his orders and left their monastery when he had specifically told them not to leave.

But the old Abbot's lecture on obedience was suddenly cut short by an older monk by the name of Brother Malcolm, who said, "You told us not to come with you because it was too dangerous, and the only reason that we should ever leave and come looking for you is if Brother John should send us to find you.

"I know you were just being sarcastic," said Brother Malcolm with a frown. "But we really did see Brother John the other night, and not only did he tell us to come and find you, he also told us where you were.

"He also gave us a letter from our local bishop granting me faculties."

The old Abbot blinked. This wasn't the first time Brother John had done something like this.

"Where's the boy?" asked Brother Malcolm as he rubbed his graying beard and looked about the cave.

Garic got up with some difficulty and went with two other monks to untie Trestan.

The boy was finally himself again, but Trestan, at first, didn't want to join the others. However, he was quickly coerced out of his hiding place by Brother Malcolm, who announced that everyone present had made an ass of themselves at one point or another in their lives, and he insisted that Trestan would be in good company with everyone else there.

This made Garic, along with some of the younger monks, laugh heartily.

The old ginger monk had so much in common with Garic that it was positively scary. That is, they were both brutally honest and unapologetically brash, but they also both had hearts of gold. In short, they were both cut from the same piece of leather.

"Come here, son," said Garic as he made a hand gesture to Trestan.

The young man obeyed and came closer to the old Deacon.

"These men are my friends, and they believe that they can help you, but it's your choice. Do you want to go with them, child?"

"Yes," said Trestan emphatically.

"Okay," said Garic, "but they have one condition."

"What's that?" asked the boy as a look of uncertainty crossed his face.

"You must first get rid of that ugly tattoo on your hand."

"But how am I to do that?" asked Trestan. "It's permanent!"

"Well," said Garic, "I know a way, but it's painful though. The question is, are you willing to suffer, child?"

"I'm willing to do anything I must to get rid of that horrible mark," said Trestan resolutely.

"Okay," said Garic. "Go get a small green log from the pile of wood that Anetta brought, and I'll help you fix your problem."

Trestan left and came back promptly with a green log.

Garic set one end of the log in the fire until the sap in it started sizzling. Then he picked it up and set the hot part of the log in Trestan's hand.

The boy closed his eyes when the log hit his hand, so he didn't see Garic grind his teeth when he also grabbed the hot part of the log.

Garic then let the log go, and it fell into the campfire.

"Why did you do that, old man?" asked the boy because he was puzzled over the fact that Garic had also willingly burned his own hand.

"I thought it was only right that I take my own medicine," said the old Deacon with a shrug.

"Girly," said Garic, "go get me the jar of ointment from my saddlebag." Anetta, who was getting quite used to Garic calling her that, quietly obeyed him.

When she came back, two of the younger monks helped Trestan bind his hand after dressing it with ointment. Once they were finished, they started helping Garic with his hand.

Father Ivan was sitting in the corner of the cave, speaking with Brother Malcolm, and when the two were done talking, Brother Malcolm announced that it was time to get the donkeys ready to leave.

Brother Malcolm took Trestan outside so that he could have a man-to-man talk with him, but before he left the cave, he told Garic, "I am leaving Alexander with you. From now on, he's your responsibility. I wash my hands of him."

A frown came to Garic's face as the old ginger monk followed Trestan outside the cave.

"What did you do this time?" asked Garic with a frown. "The last time he was that angry with you was when you and Karegan let a fox go in the kitchen."

"It wasn't the kitchen," put in the young novice whose name was Brother Christopher. "We let them go in the chapel during vespers, and it was more than one fox. I know because I helped Alexander catch them."

Garic frowned at the young man, and he went quiet.

"You're not helping things, Christopher," growled Garic, who was just a bit irritated with the young novice.

The High Prince of Merrick's face went seven shades of crimson as Garic scrutinized him.

"Well," said Garic as he raised an eyebrow at the young prince, "are you going to tell me what happened, or do I have to ask Father Malcolm?"

An awkward sort of silence fell over the place as Alexander wrapped Garic's hand in a clean strip of linen. Then, after a while, he came clean and said, "I'm afraid it's a combination of things. I'm often late for things, and I left him the other day when he took me to a village to run some errands.

"I left him so that I could talk to the miller's daughter. She's a lovely girl with a sweet face and a kind disposition. She was also engaged, but I didn't know that at the time.

"And to make things worse, her fiancé was a jealous sort of man, and he so happened to be the son of a local lord. When he caught me talking with his girl, he had me thrown into his father's dungeon.

"I was not alone, however, because Brother Christopher was with me."

"Poor Brother Malcolm," said the young novice with a sigh. "It took him nearly three days to find us."

"Yeah, and when he did, he was as grouchy as a bear with a toothache," put in Alexander with a scowl.

"When the man's father refused to let us go, Brother Malcolm promised to tear the whole place apart on the count of ten. He didn't think that Brother Malcolm was serious until he finished counting."

"I never before realized what brute strength Brother Malcolm had until that day," said Brother Christopher with a look of disbelief on his face.

"That's not the only thing I did, however," admitted Alexander sadly. "I think perhaps he may also be mad about the poem I wrote."

"I'm all ears," said Garic impatiently because he realized that Alexander was still trying to weasel out of explaining the whole story to him.

"Brother Malcolm told me to write a poem about the most beautiful and perfect woman ever born. Of course, he was talking about the Blessed Virgin, but I wrote a poem about the miller's daughter and her beautiful figure.

"And while the poem wasn't obscene, it certainly wasn't appropriate for a monk to write."

Garic gave the young prince a scowl, and Brother Christopher came to his friend's rescue by saying, "The Song of Songs is written about a beautiful woman. Why are you making such a big deal about it?"

"King Solomon was not a consecrated man of God," protested Garic.

"Neither am I, though," said the young prince.

"Were you trying to get thrown out of the Santa Della Rosa?" asked the old Deacon with a scowl.

"Yes," replied Alexander, who couldn't believe the words that were coming out of his mouth.

"Well, it did the trick," said Garic as he rubbed his beard with the tips of his fingers as if he had an itch. However, he was really just trying to keep a straight face.

"Okay," said Garic. "Now that you're no longer living at the Santa Dalo Rosa, you're going to be stuck with me.

"And from here on out, boy, you're going to sort of become my apprentice.

"Don't worry," said Garic when he saw Alexander's grimace. "I wouldn't make you take holy orders, so you can feel free to talk to as many girls as you like—just as long as they're not engaged."

Garic gave the young prince a little wink when he said this and Alexander blushed.

Father Gayorg came to tell the others that it was time to depart.

All of the men left promptly upon hearing the announcement, except for Father Ivan and Garic, who were feeling weak.

"We are going to visit a kind old widow who lives near here, and we want you and Anetta to come along as well," said Father Gayorg. "I know you're worried about her cough, and it would be beneficial to the girl if she could be out of this weather."

"I have no more strength left," said Garic. "You know what happens to me when I—"

"I understand. You're not fit to ride, but we've made both you and Father Ivan litters so that you won't have to ride a horse.

"I'm sure the old widow would be happy to have you as guests, especially if you and Alexander help her around the place until the weather gets better."

Garic agreed to come and was helped to his litter by Anetta and Alexander.

They made it to the old widow's cottage by midnight. Because Anetta insisted on walking the whole way, her feet were in terrible condition when she arrived at the old widow's cottage.

But to Anetta's great delight, she got to sleep in a worm-clean bed when they arrived at their destination.

As the night wore thin, Anetta began to dream once more about Gregor.

CHAPTER 17

Sword Dancing

he following morning, Brother Malcolm left with five companions instead of six because Brother Raul stayed behind to help take care of the old Abbot.

When Brother Malcolm said goodbye to Father Ivan, he whispered something in his ear, which left the old Abbot in stitches.

It was rather hard to tell that the two men were at all related because, with the exception of their height, they had absolutely nothing in common physically.

Brother Malcolm's mother was a barmaid, and Ivan's mother was a great lady and it clearly showed in their manners. And whatever Malcolm whispered in the old Abbotts ear was most certainly offensive to his brother Ivan, to say the least, and that's probably why Father Ivan was so amused by what he said.

"What did he say?" asked Anetta with a frown.

"It was a personal joke," explained Garic.

Anetta wasn't satisfied with the explanation, but that was the only answer the old Deacon would give her.

Garic rested for a few days, and when he felt better, he saddled his horse and went to a nearby village with Alexander to get a few things.

While they were alone, Garic took the opportunity to talk to Alexander about Anetta.

Garic began his little talk by saying, "Why don't you ever speak to Anetta? After all, you're good friends with her brother Karegan. You might even find that you like each other. And why would that be such a bad thing?"

"She won't even look at me," complained Alexander bitterly.

"You're in a habit, you goose," replied Garic with a smile. "I'm going to dress you like a nobleman. Of course, she still might not want to talk to you, but it's worth a try."

When the two men returned to the little cottage, Alexander had traded his monk's habit for clothes befitting a prince.

While they unsaddled their horses, Garic gave Alexander a pep talk on how to speak to girls, although he probably wasn't qualified for such a task.

"Now, I know you've spent most of your life in a monastery, and women are new territory for you, but what I want you to do is talk to Anetta in the same sort of way you might talk to her brother Karegan."

"Really?" said Alexander. "Girls really like that?"

"Yes," said Garic. "Actually, they really do!"

The next morning, Alexander waited by the well for Anetta to come and draw water as usual so that he could have a conversation with her.

Alexander, who approached Anetta from behind very timidly, slapped her on the back, right between the shoulders, and said, "What are you doin'?"

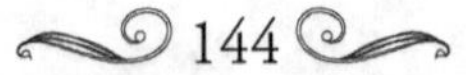

He did this simply because that's how he talked to Karegan. And in his defense, he had spent the last couple of days getting advice about women from Garic, who somehow managed to be even more awkward around the opposite sex than he was.

When he slapped Anetta on the back, she dropped her pail down the well and spun around to face Alexander. As she did so, she drew the sword that Rin had given her.

When Alexander saw Anetta's weapon, he stumbled backward, tripped over a rock, and fell into a mud puddle.

"If you ever put your hands on me again, boy, I will end you so quickly that you won't have time to blink," growled Anetta.

Alexander went back to Garic feeling quite like a failure. His clothes were soiled and wet, and his spirits were low.

However, Garic, on the other hand, was beaming with confidence, and he talked Alexander into trying again.

The next morning, Alexander was waiting by the well once more. This time, he waited right in front of the well so Anetta could not draw water unless he moved.

Anetta tried to ignore his presence, but she found that all of her efforts were futile.

Alexander didn't say a word until Anetta shoved him out of the way and filled her bucket up.

As soon as she did this, the young prince begged and pleaded with her to let him carry the bucket of water for her.

When he did this, Anetta asked, "So you think I'm incapable of doing it myself?"

"No, my lady," said Alexander. "I've just noticed that you've been limping, and I'm very much aware that you walked a long distance a few days ago. Your feet must be in a horrible condition."

"My feet are just fine," growled Anetta, who was obviously lying.

Alexander took Anetta by surprise by tackling her to the ground.

After a moment or two of rolling around in the dirt, Alexander got Anetta's shoes off.

Of course, the first thing that she did was reach for her sword. But Alexander took it and threw it as far away from her as he possibly could.

As soon as he got her shoes off her feet, he let go of her, and she went scrambling to get her sword.

But by the time Anetta reached the weapon, Alexander was already standing over the well with her shoes.

"Drop your weapon, my lady!" said Alexander. "Or your shoes will go splashing into the well."

Anetta called his bluff by taking a few steps forward while still holding the sword, but when she did so, Alexander let the shoes slip just a little bit to make his point.

Anetta was afraid that Alexander would really drop her shoes in the well, so she set her weapon down and kicked it away from herself—but only after glaring at Alexander for a moment or two.

"Okay," said Anetta. "Now, give me back my shoes."

"I don't think so," said Alexander with a mischievous grin.

"But you gave your word!" protested Anetta.

"No, I did not," said Alexander. "I only said that I wouldn't drop them in the well.

"In order to get them back... you must..."

Alexander thought very hard about how he could punish Anetta for being so difficult. After a moment or so of thought, he said, "You must first let me carry you into the cottage and let me dress your feet with ointment. I will then give your shoes back to you."

"Do you give me your word as a gentleman?" asked Anetta with a frown.

"On my honor, I will do as I said once you complete your side of the deal."

He then fished the bucket out of the well with a pole and drew fresh water to wash Anetta's feet off.

He took Anetta into the cottage and dressed her feet with oil, after which he returned her shoes promptly.

When he was finished, he went back to Garic, and just like the day before, he was covered in mud because he had rolled on the ground in the dirt. However, unlike the day before, Alexander had a look of triumph about him.

Garic would have asked what had happened, but he had seen the whole ordeal himself because he was on the roof of the little shed fixing a hole that was leaking.

While Garic was watching the two rolling around in the dirt, he got a brilliant idea.

Garic waited for a few days for Anetta's feet to heal before he asked her to give Alexander swordplay instructions.

At first, Anetta refused him flatly.

But Garic insisted that he was too tired at the end of the day to teach Alexander, and besides, Anetta had been instructed by Gregor himself. And in point of fact, Gregor was a living legend.

Garic begged Anetta for a few days before she finally gave in and agreed to teach Alexander. She did this, however, just to get rid of the old Deacon, who was an expert at annoying her.

"So how much does he know?" asked Anetta as she made Father Ivan's tea.

"Not much," said Garic just as he ducked out the door.

Anetta brought the old Abbot his brew made of bitter herbs just as soon as it was cool enough to drink. The tea helped both with Ivan's nausea and his fever.

The old cottage was small, and it only had two rooms. The largest room served both as a parlor and a kitchen.

Father Ivan slept by the hearth in the kitchen. This was the only fireplace in the little cottage.

Anetta, on the other hand, slept in the old woman's bed while the kind old lady insisted on sleeping on the floor.

This little arrangement didn't last long, however, because Anetta said something to Garic, who quickly fashioned a rough sort of bed for Anetta so that the old lady would no longer feel obliged to sleep on the floor.

Garic had also offered to build Father Ivan a bed, but the kindly old monk turned him down politely.

Because Father Ivan refused to sleep on a bed, Anetta had to kneel every time she brought Father Ivan his tea, which was really quite often recently because the fever had gotten worse.

After giving the pious old monk his tea, Anetta started making a large pot of porridge for everyone with the water that Alexander had brought in for her earlier that morning.

He had been doing that ever since the ordeal at the well, and Anetta just let him because she secretly was afraid that he would drop her shoes in the well if she said anything.

Then she'd be stuck letting him do everything for her.

After supper that day, Anetta went outside to teach Alexander how to handle a sword, and it was such an amusing sight that everyone came to watch.

In fact, even Father Ivan came sometimes to watch them.

Alexander's first five lessons were on how not to drop his sword.

Anetta taught this lesson to him by kicking the sword out of his hands and then snapping, "Go get it, boy."

The young prince was sick of this lesson by day five, and by day six, he felt rebellion bubbling up inside of him.

On the sixth day, Anetta approached him with the intention of kicking the sword out of his hand. But when she tried to do so, he dodged.

She kept coming for him, and he kept dodging her.

Finally, he tripped her, and she landed flat on her back in a puddle of mud.

Anetta got upset about her clothes being soiled, and she complained when Alexander did this.

When she complained, Alexander flung a large clod of dirt in her direction, which was easy to do because the ground was so soft that day.

Anetta, who didn't manage to dodge quickly enough, got hit square in the face with it.

She then responded with a clod of dirt of her own, which hit its mark perfectly.

Their little mud fight came to a close when Garic brought another sword into the mix.

When Anetta took the sword from Garic, Alexander let out a maniacal throat laugh.

"Rahhaaahhaa!" went the High Prince of Merrick.

Alexander waited for Anetta to come at him with her weapon.

When Anetta finally got close enough, he swung his leg behind her and tripped her.

Anetta returned the favor by kicking his feet out from underneath him and knocking him flat on his back.

Since they were both out of steam, they just lay there on their backs on the ground for a good long time, talking.

"So," said Alexander, "did you learn to use a sword because you wanted to be a man?"

"No," said Anetta as she rolled her eyes. "I learned to use the sword because I spent a year in a wine cellar being tortured on account of the fact that I was unable to protect myself."

When Anetta gave this answer, Alexander blinked. It certainly wasn't the response that he expected, and it took him completely off guard.

"So, you're some sort of Mary Elizabeth."

"What do you mean?" asked Anetta sternly.

"You know, Mary Elizabeth. You're perfect, and you can do anything without putting any effort into it. You never make a mistake or ask questions. You are just... perfect, aren't you."

Anetta let out a bout of sarcastic laughter when he said this.

"I worked hard to learn how to use the sword. I stole my brother's armor, humiliated my family in public, and I may have started a war with Merrick because I beat up King Dinithall.

"In short, I am just as imperfect as you, and I'm in the habit of making an ass of myself on a regular basis. Just like you!"

"Are you calling me an ass, my lady?" asked Alexander with a scowl.

Anetta most certainly was, and her face went red as she tried desperately to change the subject by talking about the weather.

Alexander was not offended, though. In fact, he liked that Anetta had spirit, and it made her even more interesting to him.

After that day, all of the women in Alexander's poems had dark auburn hair.

While Anetta and Alexander lay there on their backs talking to each other, Father Ivan and Garic were sitting off to one side, having a conversation of their own.

A faint smile came to Garic's lips and he found himself filled with fraternal pride as he watched Alexander talking with Anetta. In fact, they were openly flirting with each other because they didn't realize that Garic and Father Ivan could hear them. It was quite clear to the old Deacon that Alexander had finally gotten Anetta to notice him. Most girls Anetta's age met their husbands at a ball or a dance. But Anetta didn't seem to care much for those. They are sword dancing, murmured Garic under his breath.

"What are you planning on doing with the Princess Anetta of Duchaine?" asked the old Abbot with a frown. "Surely you're not still planning on leaving her in a convent after you spent so much time and effort on getting the High Prince of Merrick to notice her."

"I'm still planning on bringing her to that convent in the mountains and leaving her there, but only while I help you find Brother John," said Garic.

"Her father gave me a document stating that she's engaged, but I never signed it myself because I didn't want to start a scandal.

"If all goes well, though, I'll have Alexander sign the document."

"And there will be a strong alliance between Meric and Duchaine," said Father Ivan as a faint smile came to the old Abbot's lips. "Have you perhaps received another vision?"

The old witch hunter looked embarrassed when Ivan said this, and he responded to his question in a whisper as if he were afraid that someone else would overhear him.

"In that cave, in front of the Blessed Sacrament. I had no idea what to do with Anetta, and I felt completely lost. So I consulted my Divine Master.

"My prayers were answered by a vision. In that vision, I was shown the union between Anetta and Alexander."

"What else were you shown?" asked Father Ivan.

"Karegan will succeed his father. King Ruben will soon die, but Karegan will not have a long reign. He will name Anetta's son High Prince of Duchaine. There will be a lasting peace between Merrick and Duchaine."

"I suppose Alexander will become King of Merrick. So is King Dinithall going to die?"

"No," said Garic. "Actually, Lord Dinithall is only King Regent of Merrick, but now that Alexander is of age, he is the rightful king."

"But how are you going to get Lord Dinithall to comply and give the throne to his cousin?"

"I don't know. But it will happen somehow."

The temperature dropped gradually as the sun set that day, and as it started to get dark, everyone took shelter inside right before snowflakes started to fall.

Just as Anetta entered the little cottage, she thought she saw Lobos in the woods. But she wasn't about to let out all the warm air, so she quickly closed the door behind her.

A few moments later, however, she heard whining at the door. She opened it and let the massive grey wolfdog in.

When she did so, she sat on the ground to make herself appear small so as not to frighten him.

Lobos greeted Anetta in his usual fashion, and then he devoured a bowl of porridge that was left over from supper.

After cleaning the mud off herself, Anetta went to bed.

Anetta took Lobos to bed with her, but since Lobos didn't care much for the old woman, Anetta ended up letting him out of her room, and he curled up next to Father Ivan near the hearth. He spent most of his night there.

Anetta fell asleep quickly and started to dream.

Her dreams, however, were not pleasant ones.

The first dream she had was about Gregor, and it was the same as always, and she woke up crying.

Then she went back to sleep and dreamt that she was once again a captive in King Dinithall's wine cellar. She woke up from that dream screaming and decided that she didn't want to have another nightmare with Victor and Larson in it.

So she sought out Lobos for comfort rather than trying to go back to sleep.

When she went to get Lobos, she realized, much to her chagrin, that her screaming had woken Father Ivan.

He wanted to know what had happened that made her scream in such a way.

While Anetta tried dodging the old priest's question at first, she eventually gave in and told him all about her nightmares.

The two of them sat up in front of the hearth and talked until dawn the next day.

As the sun rose that morning, Father Ivan's high temperature returned once more, so he laid back down by the fire and fell asleep.

Father Ivan slept all day, and he only awoke when Garic came in with Alexander and Brother Raul to sing Vespers with him.

This was actually easy because Garic, who was a religious in his own right, always carried the prayers necessary for the Divine Office with him.

The little cottage echoed with their melodious voices as they sang in an ancient language, and the sound was a hauntingly beautiful one.

After Vespers, everyone left except for Garic, who was concerned about Anetta.

She already ate very little, but that day, she ate nothing. When she went to prepare supper, she fainted.

Something was obviously upsetting her, but what?

"I've tried talking to her," said Garic. "But all she said is that she will no longer be teaching Alexander how to use the sword because it's not appropriate for her to do so.

"And she insisted that it is my obligation to teach him because I sort of adopted Alexander, which makes him my son."

"I'll speak to Anetta tomorrow," said Father Ivan. "I sense that you also had something else that you wanted. So what is it?"

"I'm going to send Alexander to the village to get some things tomorrow. I want Anetta to go as well, but she wouldn't go if I told her to, so I was wondering if you would pull some strings for me."

"Are you sure that's wise?" asked the old Abbot with a frown.

"I'm sure that they'll be fine," said Garic. "Brother Raul has agreed to go with them, just as long as you're okay with him going.

"I have made all the arrangements except for asking Anetta. I get the feeling that she's depressed, and an outing will do her good."

"I'll see what I can do," said Father Ivan.

Garic knelt for Father Ivan's blessing and then left the little cottage.

As he opened the door, a small wisp of snow entered the room before Garic could close it behind him once again.

The next day, Father Ivan somehow coerced Anetta into going with Alexander and Brother Raul.

The old Deacon agreed to stay behind because Father Ivan's fever had returned, and he needed someone to stay with him.

Anetta was dressed in the old widow's finest woolen dress, and she wore a heavy wool cape with a deep hood. And to top it all off, she wore a dark gray woolen sash over her face. She was so bundled up, in fact, that it was really hard to recognize her underneath all of her layers.

Alexander, on the other hand, was dressed very much like a prince, and his dark green velvet offset his teal eyes beautifully. Alexander didn't worry much about hiding his identity because it wasn't likely that anyone would recognize him. In fact, most people who saw him just assumed that he was simply a son of a rich nobleman. This was because he had been living at the Santa Dalo Rosa most of his life.

Anetta and the old widow each rode a black gelding while Alexander rode Garic's silver mare. Brother Raul was stuck riding the little donkey to the village because the old woman had an aversion to the creatures.

When they got to the little village, they all split up because they had agreed that it was best for them to go their own ways and then meet up in the village square at noon. After leaving the local wool merchant, Alexander and Anetta headed for the village square so that they could meet up with their companions.

Garic had given Alexander his signet ring because the High Prince of Merrick was planning on proposing to Anetta. She knew that Alexander was up to something, and when she saw him playing with

Garic's ring, which he had in his pocket, she knew exactly what he was planning.

This situation made Anetta uncomfortable, and her discomfort got even worse when Alexander approached her and removed a strand of hair from her face.

For the first time, Anetta did not withdraw from his hand, but this was partly because she was so distracted by her own thoughts, and she was desperately trying to think up a way to let Alexander down easy.

Anetta had always before looked at romance at a distance, but never before had she found herself in the midst of it. When she realized the sort of situation that she was in, she was terrified. In fact, the real reason that Anetta didn't want to teach Alexander swordplay lessons was because she was starting to notice him as a man. While this was only natural, and Anetta's modesty was a good thing, shutting Alexander out completely was perhaps going just a little bit overboard. But after her past experiences with men, though, who could really blame her?

As Alexander reached inside his pocket for the ring, he was brimming with confidence. His day seemed to be going perfectly. Anetta hated herself for what she was about to do because she was going to turn down Alexander's offer of marriage flatly, and she was sure to crush Alexander with her refusal.

Just before Alexander could pull Garic's signet ring out of his pocket, he saw Brother Raul coming around the corner. He had his sleeves rolled up to his elbows, and for the first time, Alexander noticed that the monk had a pentagram tattoo on his forearm.

When he noticed this, he took Anetta by surprise by picking her up, setting her on the back of Garic's silver mare, and slapping the horse in the hindquarters. When Alexander did this, the horse took off like a flash of light and carried Anetta far away from harm.

Just as the silver mare disappeared with Anetta on her back, several assassins, all dressed in black, stepped into the village square. They each had a drawn sword. Now, the one thing Anetta managed to drill into his head was that there are about a hundred ways to make your opponent drop their weapon. However, he was unarmed and outnumbered; therefore, he was eventually captured.

The silver mare was jumpy, and she threw Anetta before she reached the little cottage.

When Garic saw his horse come back without a rider, he didn't think anything of it because he knew just how jumpy she was. In fact, Garic was perfectly at ease until Lackmore came rushing into the cottage, carrying Anetta, who was unconscious...

CHAPTER 18

Finding Karegan

ackmore, who was driven by concern for his sister Ella, rode his horse like a madman and got to his mother's cottage before Michellie did. But when he got there, all he found was a note stating that his sister would be returned once he cut the head off the High Prince Karegan.

This letter was signed: Lord Doomlock, Prince of Darkness.

Lackmore got back on his horse and went in search of the High Prince of Duchaine so that he could save his sister from a fate worse than death.

The palace guard was obviously not thinking straight because if he was, he would never have believed that Doomlock would give Ella back unharmed after he killed the High Prince Karegan.

Doomlock was a master of manipulation, though, and Lackmore, at this point, desperately wanted to save his sister Ella.

He was so desperate, in fact, that all reason had gone from him.

Just as soon as Lackmore left, Drago arrived.

This was because Victor had sent him to follow Lackmore and kill him as soon as he cut the head off Prince Karegan.

For you see, no one says no to their coven, and if all went as planned by Doomlock, there would be no one left to save the Fair Lady Ella.

But since the sinister powers of darkness aren't the only thing at work in the world and good always conquers evil, there was still much reason to hope.

However, Lackmore had given himself over to darkness for such a long period of time that he had completely forgotten about Divine Providence.

So it only stood to reason that when he was faced with a crisis situation, he only depended upon himself and not his Divine Master.

When Michellie arrived and entered Ella's home, Drago hid himself.

He wasn't expecting Michellie, and Michellie was expecting Victor and maybe even Larson to show up.

But never in his wildest dreams would Michellie have thought that Drago would be sent there instead to kill Lackmore.

Drago left his hiding place because he somehow got it in his head that he would make a name for himself by killing the man dubbed "The Reaper" by the Seven Covens.

When Michellie saw Drago step out of the shadows, he instantly knew what he was there for, and his face went white with horror.

"Ohh, my son, what have you done to yourself?" asked Michellie.

Now, if Drago had any of his humanity left, he would have felt at least a small stab of remorse when he saw just how grief-stricken Michellie was when he realized that he had completely ruined himself.

But he had no more humanity left in him, and so it mattered very little to him.

Drago approached Michellie, and if Michellie had followed his instinct, he would have drawn his sword and cut Drago's head off his shoulders long before the other man could act.

But Michellie hesitated, and when he did draw his sword and cut off Drago's head, it was too late because Drago had thrown a poisoned dagger at him.

And while the dagger did not wound Michellie mortally, its blade was dipped in a poison that had no antidote.

Michellie pulled the dagger out of his shoulder and left the cottage.

But as he started to mount his horse, he suddenly noticed Lord Roslyn lying dead on the ground, and he couldn't just leave him there, so he pulled him up on his saddle next to him.

He then spurred his horse and took off.

Michellie's death sentence had been signed the moment he was stabbed by Drago's poisoned dagger, and he only had a little time left to warn the High Prince Karegan of Lackmore's treachery.

He didn't need to read Doomlock's letter to know what Lackmore was planning.

Lackmore had a head start, and his horse was only carrying one man.

Michellie's horse was carrying two men, but Michellie was one of the best trackers ever born, and his skill as a horseman was only rivaled by Garic.

He also knew almost every inch of land between Meric and Duchaine, and that included the Great Mountains and the Daroogian Forest.

It was because of his superior knowledge and skill that Michellie ended up in front of Lackmore despite the other advantages he had over Michellie.

Of course, Michellie could have hunted down Lackmore, but that wouldn't have solved the problem because Victor and Larson were still alive, and they were going to make sure the High Prince Karegan died.

And since Michellie was dying as well, the very best he could do was warn Karegan that they were coming for him because his time was so limited.

Lackmore got lost after just a few days in the woods, and when he no longer knew where he was going, he started following Michellie's trail.

This was really quite easy to do because, despite Michellie's best efforts to hide his tracks, the poison was killing him slowly, and it was making him very sick.

Lackmore started to believe that Michellie was also lost, but he quickly changed his mind when he passed through a small village, and the people there spoke of two ginormous men with blonde hair who had slain a horde of witch assassins to protect a quiet stranger who traveled with them.

Lackmore knew beyond a shadow of a doubt that the quiet stranger was, in fact, the High Prince Karegan and the two giants were Dimitri and Malkovich.

This confirmed that Michellie was riding in the right direction.

They were gaining on Karegan and his companions when it started to snow.

This made things much more difficult for the two men, but not impossible.

During the great snowstorm, Michellie managed to put a great deal of distance between himself and Lackmore because Karegan and his companions had stopped to take shelter from the weather.

Michellie almost caught up with Karegan before he lost consciousness and fell off his horse.

When Dimitri and Malkovich realized that they were being followed, they both went to see who it was.

To their great surprise, they found Roslyn dead on the ground, and next to him was Michellie, who had fainted and was, therefore, unable to tell them about the impending threat of danger that hung over their heads.

The two men decided to split up.

Malkovich stayed behind to bury Lord Roslyn while Dimitri took Michellie and put him on his horse.

After meeting up with the High Prince, who was waiting for them, they decided to take Michellie to a nearby cottage where a kind old widow lived so that the man could be cared for.

The old widow was a member of Father Ivan's third order, and she was dedicated to helping people in need.

Michellie was running a high temperature, and he needed to be looked after.

Lackmore found Anetta unconscious on the ground and decided to take her to the same cottage.

Since Dimitri and Malkovich were held up for a while when they buried Lord Roslyn, Lackmore beat everyone to the little cottage.

When Lackmore came rushing through the door, holding Anetta in his arms, he was the very picture of distress.

Garic, who was sitting on the floor by the hearth next to Father Ivan, got up instantly when Lackmore came rushing in and asked, "What happened?"

"I don't know," said Lackmore as he laid Anetta on the floor gently and tried to revive her.

When he realized that Garic was gripping the hilt of his sword tightly, as if he was considering whether or not to cut his head off, he said, "I found her on the side of the road like this."

And since Garic still didn't let go of his hilt, Lackmore added, "I would never do anything to hurt her."

Lackmore blinked when he said this, for he suddenly realized that if he did indeed kill Karegan, it would destroy Anetta.

Garic saw Lackmore blink, and he was sure that the man was somehow lying to him.

It wasn't long before Anetta regained consciousness, and when she opened her eyes, Father Ivan, Garic, and Lackmore were all standing over her.

Just then, Dimitri came bursting through the door.

He had left Michellie outside with Karegan, and he drew his sword as he took long strides toward Lackmore.

If Garic wouldn't kill him, then Dimitri would.

Michellie was very close friends with Dimitri despite the fact that their personalities clashed horribly, and the bodyguard was sure that Lackmore was responsible for what had happened to his friend.

Before Dimitri could reach the palace guard, however, Karegan also came rushing through the door and said in a loud voice, "Dimitri! Go outside and bring Michellie in out of the cold."

Dimitri, who was always promptly obedient to his High Prince, hesitated to obey him for the very first time.

Dimitri gave Garic a quiet look of worry, then left.

Garic didn't let go of the hilt of his sword until his hand was slapped by Father Ivan.

"What happened to you, sis?" asked Karegan with a frown.

"I got thrown off my horse," said Anetta as she put her hand to her head, which was throbbing.

She then sighed and said, "Lackmore found me, and he must have brought me here."

"My friend, please step outside with me," said Karegan as he turned to leave.

Lackmore tried to follow him, but he was stopped by Anetta, who grabbed his hand.

"I'm grateful for all you have done, and your dedication and loyalty to my brother mean the world to me. I know you would willingly lay down your life for Karegan if he were ever in danger."

Anetta squeezed Lackmore's hand so hard when she said the word danger that it sort of hurt a little.

Lackmore turned to leave because he was upset, and he did not want Anetta to see it.

Karegan was waiting for him just behind the little barn.

The High Prince Karegan embraced Lackmore as if they were the dearest of friends when they met behind the barn.

When he did so, he whispered, "Take me deep into the woods and do what you must. But don't let my sister see it. She won't understand."

Karegan then let go of his friend's shoulders, and when he did so, Lackmore noticed Dimitri and Malkovich staring at him intently.

The two men looked like two blue-eyed hawks watching their prey.

Karegan walked slowly towards the woods with Lackmore.

When the two men left, Malkovich wanted to follow them, but Dimitri stopped him.

Instead of following Karegan, the two men took Michellie inside so that his wound could be dressed.

Upon entering the little cottage, they saw Garic stringing his bow and arguing with Anetta because she wanted to come with him.

When they laid Michellie down, he woke up and refused to let his wound be dressed, insisting that the High Prince was in grave peril.

Michellie was such a big man that there was no way to make him cooperate with them, so he ended up going outside with Garic.

As Garic turned to leave, he took Anetta's sword from her and promised that if she dared leave the cottage, he would bind her hand and foot and lock her in the old widow's bedroom.

Just before Dimitri ducked out the door, he called Anetta over to him and handed her one of his own short-bladed swords.

"Now don't wander off, child, or Garic will burst a blood vessel," he told her.

Anetta walked back to the hearth, holding Dimitri's sword as if it were a trophy, and she had a look of triumph about her as she joined Father Ivan.

Garic followed Dimitri out to the woods, and he glared at the bodyguard as he walked.

He said nothing, yet the look on his face screamed, you traitor.

When Michellie finally found Karegan, he was standing in front of Lackmore.

The two men just stood there staring at each other.

Lackmore had his sword drawn, but it would have been just as easy for the palace guard to kill his own sister, Ella, as it would be to kill Karegan.

As they stood there in the snow-like living statues amongst the leafless trees, the sun began to set.

Lackmore sheathed his sword as if to say to his friend, You win.

Just as he did this, though, Larson came out of nowhere with the poison dagger that was intended for the High Prince.

Lackmore turned to face Larson, took three steps, and then buried the poisoned dagger in his own chest.

After which, he unsheathed his sword again and cut Larson's head clean off his shoulders with one stroke of his blade.

After this, Lackmore fell face down on the ground.

As he fell, several other assassins appeared in the distance and could be seen moving through the trees of the forest.

When Michellie saw Victor, he whispered, "He's mine."

Michellie was so weak that he had to put an arm around Garic for support.

When he saw Victor, though, he let go of Garic's shoulders.

The first step he took towards Victor was a rather clumsy one because the man was slowly dying, and he was incredibly weak.

However, the next three steps he took were like poetry in motion, so graceful was his movement, and at the third step, he drew his sword and cut Victor's head clean off his shoulders.

The moment Victor's head hit the ground, Michellie's heart stopped on account of the poison, and he fell dead to the ground beside Victor.

He had spent the very last of his strength completing his mission, which was given to him by his High Prince.

And while an ordinary man could not have done what he had, Michellie was no ordinary man.

It wasn't long before the other assassins started getting close enough to be a threat.

Garic started picking them off with arrows.

Dimitri and Malkovich, who also had bows of their own, quickly began doing the same as Garic.

All three men were deadly with their bows, and since the moon was full that night, they had plenty of light.

They eventually ran out of arrows, so they resorted to using their swords.

The battle came to an end just before the sun rose the next morning, and while Garic, Dimitri, and Malkovich stayed outside to bury the dead, the High Prince Karegan was sent inside to rest.

This made him rather unhappy, but he was outnumbered by his friends, so he gave in and went inside.

When Garic turned one of the men over, whom he had shot with an arrow, he was shocked to find that the man was only a boy, about Trestan's age.

As the old Deacon sank to his knees and emptied his stomach, he was sharply reminded of why he hunted down people like Victor and Larson, who were dedicated to destroying the innocence of the young.

Although no one said it, it was clearly written on everyone's face.

This wasn't a mere power struggle—it was a battle for the youth.

Michellie's body was the last one to be buried.

To everybody's great surprise, Lackmore was still barely alive when they had finished burying the others.

Garic ran into the cottage in order to fetch Father Ivan so that the palace guard could receive the sacraments before he died.

Instead of taking Father Ivan to the place where Lackmore lay, though, he sent Karegan to do it.

So far, all Anetta had told Garic was that she had been thrown by the silver mare.

Garic had so many questions welling up inside of him, and since he was so busy the day before, there was no time to ask questions.

This was his first opportunity to figure out what happened to Anetta's companions.

She broke out in tears when Garic mentioned Alexander, and it took her a few moments to calm down.

But once she composed herself, she told the old Deacon what had happened the day before.

While he was leading Father Ivan, Karegan suddenly had a vision. Because his sight failed him, he was forced to sit down while his vision lasted.

But Father Ivan barely stopped because Malkovich soon came to show him to the place where the palace guard lay.

Dimitri wanted to bring Lackmore inside on account of the cold, but since he was barely alive, Garic was afraid that he would die before they could bring him inside.

So they all took off their cloaks and covered the dying man with them.

They also built a little bonfire for Lackmore as well.

As the good monk approached the dying man, he noticed that he was holding something peculiar in his hand.

"Where did you get that?" asked Father Ivan as he pointed to the cross that Brother John had given Lackmore.

"The man who ruined my life gave it to me," said Lackmore with a little bout of sarcastic laughter, which died quickly because it hurt him to laugh.

"My son," said the old priest sternly, "there isn't much time left for you, so let me hear your confession before it's too late."

Malkovich, when he realized that Lackmore was about to make his last confession, left quickly.

Just as soon as he had gone, the palace guard did make his confession, and because he had spent so much time away from his Divine Master, his confession was a lengthy one.

After giving absolution to Lackmore, Father Ivan gave him the Blessed Sacrament.

But when he was about to anoint him, the palace guard complained of being cold, so the kindly old priest wrapped the dying man in his own cloak, sat on the ground with him, and rocked him back and forth while singing the Salve Regina in a low tone of voice.

The old Abbot looked much like a mother comforting a very big, tired boy.

When Father Ivan was halfway through his song, however, he suddenly realized that Lackmore had died.

Father Ivan felt a sad sort of joy as he laid Lackmore down on the ground and covered his face with the corner of his cloak.

He never stopped singing, though, until he had finished his song.

Father Ivan headed back to the cottage and curled up next to the hearth. He dozed off quickly by the warmth of the fireplace, and he slept for an hour or so because he was completely worn out.

Karegan sat by the well while Dimitri went to fetch Anetta so that her brother could speak to her.

He then went to help Malkovich take Lackmore's body into the barn so that the wild animals wouldn't carry it off while they went to get something to eat.

He then joined the others at the table in the parlor.

Garic fell asleep at the table while talking to Anetta.

Karegan waited patiently by the well for his sister to finish making a pot of porridge for everyone.

When Anetta was finally finished in the kitchen, she went to see what Karegan wanted.

To her great surprise, Karegan started babbling much like Brother John did when he had one of his visions.

When Anetta went back to the cottage, everyone was snoring, including Dimitri and Malkovich.

She went over to Father Ivan, who was sleeping, and took him a cup of tea because he was burning up once again with fever.

"Father, please release me from an oath I have taken. I'm sure Garic won't, especially considering what I'm about to do."

"I release you, my child," said Father Ivan. "Now, if you kneel, I'll give you a general absolution just because I get the sense that you're about to do something that's terribly dangerous."

When she got up off her knees, Father Ivan sighed deeply because he knew full well that he might never see Anetta again.

When she opened the door to leave, she let in a cold draft, which made the old Abbot feel numb.

Not cold or sad—just numb.

CHAPTER 19

Summoned

When Garic awoke, everyone else was already up.

"Where is Anetta?" asked Garic as he glanced around the room briefly.

He was obviously talking to Father Ivan, but the old Abbot ignored him as he vested himself for mass. This was despite the fact that he was feeling really quite terribly ill. Karegan answered Garic in his place.

"I asked her to take care of the horses because you were exhausted," said the High Prince as he added another log to the dying fire.

Of course, Karegan wasn't telling the whole truth, but the last thing he wanted was for Garic to go running off after Anetta. He knew full well that the old Deacon would only get himself killed by Doomlock if he did so. When Father Ivan saw Garic putting on his cloak and boots, he stopped him by placing a hand on his shoulder and said, "Please stay until the end of mass, my son. After that, there will be plenty of time for you to find Alexander."

Father Ivan was never told that Anetta had been sent by her brother Karegan to kill Doomlock and bring back the High Prince of Merrick, but the old Abbot wasn't stupid either, and he had a pretty good idea of what Anetta was up to as well. The little kitchen table was quickly transformed into an altar. Garic sort of lost consciousness in the middle of mass because he had another one of his visions, and he remained there for nearly an hour afterward. He wasn't able to do much when the vision ended because he was completely out of strength, and this often happened after one of his ordeals.

He did try to leave, however, to bring Anetta back because he suddenly realized that she had gone. However, he collapsed just outside the door of the little cottage, and he had to be brought back in by Dimitri, who laid him on one of the beds in the old widow's room. And for the first time in a very long time, the old Deacon spent the night in a real bed.

Garic was awakened the next morning by Karegan, who was holding an earthen bowl full of porridge. When Garic refused to eat, Karegan took the wooden spoon and started trying to feed him as if he were a small child.

"Come on, old man," said Karegan. "Don't be stubborn!"

As he said this, he held a spoonful of food under Garic's nose.

"Why didn't you tell me that she left?" asked Garic bitterly.

"Because you're a mule, and if I told you, you would not have come back. At least this way, you both have a fighting chance of surviving. You must eat so that you can regain your strength."

Garic finally did take a bite, and as he chewed, he frowned and asked, "Who made the porridge today?"

"I did," said Karegan as he scooped up another spoonful of porridge for Garic. But as he brought the spoon closer to the old Deacon's mouth, Garic took it and started eating on his own. As he chewed his porridge, he scowled at Karegan as if to accuse him of burning it, but he said nothing as he chewed up a chunk of charcoal in his food.

"I'm sorry I scorched it," said Karegan, who was embarrassed. "Dimitri and Malkovich discovered that Lackmore's body was gone, and they called me outside to help them look for him. When I came back, the porridge was sticking to the bottom of the pot."

"It's not bad, though, once you get past the crunchy pieces," said Garic in an attempt to make Karegan feel better about burning it.

"Two men from your order came earlier this morning. They were hunting the men who attacked us the other night. They are still here because they wish to speak to you. I'll help you walk to the table, but I wanted you to eat something first before you went and saw them."

After saying this, Karegan reached into a pocket and, pulled out a piece of parchment paper and handed it to Garic. Anetta had written care instructions for the old Deacon, and Karegan thought it was hilarious. Garic, however, found it quite a bit less amusing than Karegan did. But the old Deacon did chuckle softly when he read the note.

After handing the note back to Karegan, Garic said, "Please don't let Dimitri or Malkovich see this. They will never let me live this down."

As soon as Garic finished eating, Karegan helped him walk to the table where two men sat. One of them was a priest, and the other one was a deacon like Garic. They were both dressed plainly in gray wool clothes. Father Talisman was in his fifties, like Garic. He had short black hair and a receding hairline. His eyes were large and dark blue, and he was clean-shaven. His hair was graying, and he was quite a bit taller than Garic. He was thin and broad-shouldered. He didn't wear a sword like his companion, but he did have a short dagger strapped to his belt. That was only because the rule of Garic's order required him to wear a weapon of some sort, and a short dagger was the minimum allowed.

Talisman's companion was a tall, gray-eyed blond, but he was only twenty-five years of age. He had a square face and broad shoulders as well. His name was Larimic, and unlike Father Talisman, he wore a cross-hilt sword strapped to his back. He was clean-shaven with short-cropped hair. Both men were dressed almost exactly like Garic. When they saw their superior approaching the table, they both stood up, but as soon as Garic sat down, both men took their seats once more.

"We are leaving just as soon as Dimitri and Malkovich get the horses ready."

"Where are we going?" asked Garic.

"We are going to Saint Wenceslas until you recover. Then you and I will go get Anetta, Alexander, and Ella back from Doomlock. Larimic will take Father Ivan to Merrick to retrieve Brother John, and after that, we will start working on putting Alexander on his father's throne."

Garic was Father Talisman's superior. However, Father Talisman was Garic's confessor, and the old deacon would have jumped off a cliff if Father Talisman told him to.

"The High Prince of Duchaine is coming with us because it is no longer safe to stay here," said Father Talisman with a scowl. "We have Brother Raul's treachery to thank for that, though."

Of course, Garic was not able to ride his horse, and so both he and Father Ivan rode on litters the whole way. Their trip took a whole week when it normally should have taken only a day or two. This was partly because Father Ivan and Garic both had to ride on litters the whole way. This was also partly because Karegan insisted on taking a detour.

Saint Wenceslas was a little convent in the mountains, and it was the very same one where Anetta was supposed to have been left. It was a day's journey from the Santa Dalo Rosa. It took Karegan a considerable amount of time to talk his companions into taking the detour, but they were glad that they listened to him in the end because they discovered that Brother Malcolm and his companions had been attacked by a group of witch assassins.

Everyone was dead except for Trestan, who had been taken captive, and Brother Christopher, who had been knocked unconscious by Brother Malcolm when he realized they were being attacked by assassins. All the monks except for Brother Christopher had been killed. Because his face was covered in blood, he appeared to be dead, but he was only unconscious. However, when he came to, he got stuck burying his dead companions. Since the ground was frozen, it was taking longer than it normally would have in warmer weather.

When Karegan and his companions came across Brother Christopher, the poor novice was completely distraught with grief. It didn't take long for Karegan and his companions to finish burying the dead, and since Garic and Father Ivan were unable to help the others, they occupied themselves by comforting Brother Christopher, who was positively distraught.

They spent the night in a grove of evergreens, and the next day, they arrived at the convent at noon. Garic spent the night there, and to his great delight, the porridge wasn't burnt this time because it was not made by Karegan but rather by the nuns. After eating breakfast, he and Father Talisman left in pursuit of Lady Anetta. Before Garic departed, Brother Christopher exchanged his monk's habit for a sword and plain gray clothes like the ones worn by the men in Garic's order. Christopher was now a novice in Garic's order, and he longed to avenge his dead brothers. The High Prince Karegan warned Garic not to let the young man into his order because he saw darkness growing in his heart. But Garic paid no heed to Karegan's warning.

That afternoon, a messenger arrived and informed the High Prince Karegan that his father had died. The messenger's name was Arlo. This man was the second son of the Grand Duke and cousin to the High Prince Karegan. Arlo had tried to join the palace guards when he was only fourteen, but he was told to go home to his mother by Gregor.

Arlo came back, however, a year later, and he was more eager than ever to join the palace guard. But Lord Gregor sent him away a second time and told him only to come back when he had hair on his chest.

Now, what Gregor really meant was that Arlo should come back only when he was of age. The youngest age for the palace guard was nineteen and no younger. But Arlo took Gregor seriously when he said that he needed chest hair in order to be a palace guard. So when Arlo turned seventeen, he came back to the captain of the palace guard and showed him his little patch of chest hair by taking off his shirt.

Both Gregor and Michellie were quite amused by the little incident, and they both laughed so hard that they almost fell off their seats. Gregor gave in to Arlo that day and gave him a uniform. He also enlisted the young man in the ranks of the palace guard. But Gregor refused to give Arlo a sword, and he wouldn't let him stand guard either. Instead, Arlo quickly became everyone's errand boy.

Now, while this wasn't quite what Arlo had in mind, at least he was allowed to wear the uniform. That was a small victory, but a victory nonetheless.

When the palace guard approached Karegan, he got down on one knee and exclaimed in a dramatic tone of voice while pressing one fist to his heart, "My most sovereign Prince, you have been summoned."

At this point, Karegan could take no more, and he rushed over to his cousin, grabbed him by the shoulders, and raised him up off his knees, squeezing him so hard that Arlo thought his head was going to pop off his shoulders.

"Your father's dead! Your mother needs you at home!" gasped Arlo as he struggled to free himself from his cousin's grip.

Karegan released his grip on Arlo when he realized what he had just said. A pain shot through his very soul as he loosened his grip, and Arlo went stumbling back because he didn't expect it, but he quickly caught his balance.

Karegan turned around, sat down on the floor, and wept bitter tears over the loss of his father.

When the High Prince Karegan regained his composure, he turned to Dimitri, but he didn't say a word. The bodyguard, however, seemed to read his mind and said, "I will make ready our horses, and we will leave for home at once."

Just as soon as Dimitri left, Karegan turned to his cousin and said, "I have a mission for you, Arlo. You will have to forego attending my coronation. What I'm about to ask of you is a great honor, though."

"Your wish is my command," said Arlo as he tried to bow again.

But Karegan stopped him and said, "If you keep on insisting on groveling before me, I will noogie you so hard that you'll go completely bald. I'm your kinsman, not just your prince. I want you to help Lord Laremec take Father Ivan to Merrick and bring Brother John back to the Santa Dalo Rosa."

Arlo was just a bit disappointed at first. However, he was so excited that Lord Laremec promised to teach him swordplay that he completely forgot about his disappointment. When Karegan left for home, he made sure that Arlo finally got a sword of his own.

Father Ivan was so ill that they were going to be stuck at Saint Wenceslas almost until spring, though. Until then, Arlo and Laremec were simply going to stay in the nuns' little guesthouse, and they would repay the kindness of the nuns by doing little odd jobs around the place.

When Karegan got home, he found the Queen Mother in deep mourning. The coronation took place just days after his father's funeral. The sides of Karegan's head were then shaved, and his remaining hair was put into a long, intricate braid that hung halfway down his back. This made him look even more like his father.

King Ruben was a just man and a great ruler, and it clearly showed both in his family and in his kingdom. Everyone showed up to his funeral. Even his worst enemies were there. In fact, there were so many mourners at his funeral that not even the great cathedral of the capital city of Duchaine could accommodate everyone that came.

After a couple of weeks, things started to slow down, and finally, after week three, Karegan was able to sit quietly by himself and drink a cup of tea. Of course, Dimitri and Malkovich still insisted on being in the room with him at all times. This was probably because Karegan's father was assassinated by one of the maids. Dimitri and Malkovich didn't trust anybody alone with Karegan anymore, and he couldn't make them leave, no matter what he said or how much he threatened them.

Karegan sat quietly, drinking his tea, when he suddenly called Dimitri over.

"You must go find Anetta," said Karegan. "She will need you before long, little one. I want you to go and protect Anetta with your life."

At first, Dimitri thought that Karegan was just trying to get rid of him. Then, he suddenly realized that the king was babbling.

"But, your majesty—" protested the old bodyguard.

Karegan stopped him mid-sentence, however, by imposing silence on him with a hand gesture.

"Lackmore will soon be here, so I will no longer be in need of your protection. You must find Anetta, little one, and defend her with your last breath. Farewell, my good and faithful servant. Your loyalty has given me great comfort."

When Karegan was done speaking, Dimitri left promptly in search of Anetta.

CHAPTER 20

Hunting Doomlock

netta stood by the well in front of Karegan, who was sitting on the ground. The High Prince looked up at his sister and said, "Ride into the Great Mountains for a day. Then, turn your horse to the west. The terrain is rough, so it will take you a while. It should be easy for you to find Doomlock's castle because its black spires are so unique, and they stand out quite vividly against the snow-capped mountains."

"Why me?" asked Anetta. "Why not Garic, Dimitri, or Malkovich? In fact, just about anyone else would be more suited to this task than I am. I couldn't even kill King Dinithall when I had a chance, and he was such an easy target. How on earth am I to kill Doomlock?"

"Mercy is never a weakness, little one," said Karegan with a sigh.

Anetta blinked back tears when he said this. The last time her brother had called her that was right before she was sent to Merrick, to the Queen's Royal Court, and Karegan predicted that she would be called to suffer atrocities. That was the first time that Anetta realized that her brother had the gift of prophecy. It was also the first time that she had ever heard anyone babble. Of course, Garic and Father Ivan were also visionaries as well, but for them, it was usually quite a bit different than it was for Karegan and Brother John.

Anetta suddenly realized that Karegan was still talking. She tried her best to listen to him, although she was very distracted. Anetta caught most of what he was saying to her.

"First of all," he said, "you must find the aviary and set the two doves and the red falcon free. But no matter what you do or how much he begs you, do not release the golden finch. Try not to touch anything if it is not completely necessary, and kill Doomlock as soon as possible. You were charged with this task not because of any physical ability of yours but because of your kindness and purity of heart.

"Take our father's sword and his armor. Go into the mountains and slay the one who calls himself the Prince of Darkness. Only take care. There is a dreadful curse on that place, and there is no telling what manner of depravity you might find there. Make haste! You only have a small amount of time left to save our friends."

Anetta got Father Ivan's general absolution, then she went to the little barn and saddled up Karegan's horse. The horse that Karegan rode was a chestnut stallion, and this horse was even faster than Garic's silver mare. After the horse was ready, she put on her brother's armor. However, she took a moment to visit the place where Lackmore's body lay.

To her great consternation, though, his body wasn't there anymore. She knelt anyway and said an **Ave** for his peaceful repose.

As Anetta rode off, she puzzled over the fact that Lackmore's body had vanished. He was locked in a little stall of the barn, and no wild animal should have been able to carry him away. Yet his body was gone. It was as if he had gotten up and ridden off on his own horse.

Lobos followed Anetta into the Great Mountains, and Anetta was grateful for his company on her lonely quest, for she felt quite forlorn all by herself. After a few days in the Great Mountains, Anetta took refuge in a cave because it started to snow, and she was very much alone with her own thoughts.

While she waited in the cave for the blizzard to pass, she started to mourn her dead friends. Michellie had always been exceedingly kind to Anetta, and she would dearly miss him. Lackmore, despite his many faults, would also be terribly missed by Anetta and everyone else who knew him. She knew full well that she would probably be the one who would have to tell poor Ella about her brother's death, and she certainly was not looking forward to it. Lackmore was just about all Ella had left after her father died.

Poor girl, thought Anetta as she roasted a squirrel that Lobos had caught for her.

Anetta didn't feel much like eating, though her stomach growled at her. She just felt cold, and it was the same cold that Michellie felt right before he died. Anetta got as close to the fire as she could, but this did not help with the cold she felt. It only made her cheeks go red.

Anetta knew full well that priests give people general absolutions when they are in grave danger of death. She also remembered Brother John telling her to prepare to die. So, was she going to die? Had she perhaps been sent on a suicide mission?

Anetta was exhausted, so she fell asleep quickly that night, and to her great delight, she slept so hard that she had no dreams. No night terrors with Victor and Larson in them, either. In fact, she didn't dream at all that night.

After staying in the cave for a few days while the storm passed, Anetta was on her way once more. She walked a lot, and it really didn't slow down her travel much because the terrain was so rough that her horse was going at a snail's pace anyway. However, this manner of travel was exceedingly hard on her feet, and after a few days of walking, Anetta was forced to ride the horse once more because her feet were in such terrible shape that she could hardly stand on them without experiencing a great deal of pain.

After a while, Doomlock's castle could be seen in the distance, and this was long before Anetta was anywhere near it because it was built on top of a mountain. It was made of black stones dug from a quarry near the Black River, and that's probably where it got its signature color.

Anetta's skin crawled the first time she saw the ginormous structure in the distance, and this feeling only got worse as she grew closer to it.

Finally, after what seemed like forever, Anetta approached a great drawbridge, but Lobos let out a little whimper, and he refused to follow her past this point. Coward murmured to Anetta when she realized that he wasn't going to go any further. She crossed herself as she rode her horse over the drawbridge as quickly as she could. She just couldn't wait to finish her quest so that she could leave the place. The very air seemed to have an unnatural chill about it, and she kept getting the unsettling feeling that she was being watched by unseen eyes, but every time she turned around, there was no one there.

When she came to a massive door, which was the main entrance, thunder crashed, and it began to rain. Since it was so cold, the rain started to freeze on the ground. As she reached for the great brass hoop that served as a doorknob, Anetta suddenly remembered that Karegan had told her to take the narrow way.

Anetta found what she was looking for quite easily, but when she tried to open the door, she discovered that it was locked. She looked for the key but was unable to find it. So she simply took the main entrance.

This was Anetta's first mistake.

She hardly took two steps before she fell straight through the floor. If she had simply looked a bit harder, she would have found the key was hidden in plain sight. However, she was simply too impatient, so she ended up falling through the floor and landing on top of a massive table in a large banquet hall.

The only visible injury she sustained was a broken ankle. However, she did hit her head really hard when she landed on the tabletop.

Anetta lay on her back for a moment or two before she suddenly realized that she had found the aviary where Doomlock kept every sort of bird imaginable.

Anetta loved birds, but her hair stood on end when they all started crying out to her in human voices. They begged her to free them, and her heart started breaking because of their sorrowful pleading.

Anetta was so distracted that she had completely forgotten Karegan's warning. After setting the falcon and the two doves free, she started letting all the other birds go as well.

There was every kind of bird in Doomlock's aviary. There were pigeons, doves, and sparrows. There were also cardinals and ravens. There was even a ginormous golden eagle in the corner of the room. To her great surprise, she found there were also exotic birds from faraway places. There were peacocks and pheasants as well. Anetta let most of them go.

When she was finished, all the birds had been released, with the exception of the golden finch and the creepy owl, which was chained up in the corner. It could have just been Anetta's imagination, but she could have sworn that the owl's eyes glowed red when she walked past it while setting the others free. It gave her the creeps, and she made a point not to release it.

Every chain, padlock, and cage in the place was more or less rusted, except for the ones that held the two doves and the red falcon. These birds were, in fact, Ella, Alexander, and Trestan—trapped in animal form by a terrible curse. The reason their cages and chains had no rust was because there was still time to save them from their enchantment. But once their cages and chains became rusted, they would be stuck in the form of birds until they died.

The eagle had been in his form so long that the chain and padlock that held him were rusted so badly that they almost crumbled when Anetta tried to smash them.

All the birds Anetta freed, with the exception of Alexander, Ella, and Trestan, flew away, and the great golden eagle was no exception. But before he left, he warned Anetta not to set the golden finch free.

You would think that she would have listened to him, especially since the High Prince had given her the same advice. However, the golden finch was enchanted, and as soon as Anetta looked at him, a spell was cast upon her. She couldn't help but let him go.

Once he was free, the only bird left in chains was the creepy owl in the corner with the glowing red eyes. But that was soon remedied by the finch.

For as soon as Anetta let him go, he grabbed the great chain around the owl's neck, and as he did so, it disappeared in a cloud of smoke that smelled like sulfur.

The moment the owl was set free, it turned into a ginormous cobra, and all hell seemed to break loose as it started to chase Anetta.

Since she had broken her ankle when she fell, Anetta wasn't able to run very fast because she was forced to hobble. The fact that her feet were in such bad condition from all the walking she had done didn't help anything either.

Soon, Anetta tripped, and just when she thought it was all over and the snake was going to swallow her hole, the great Eagle returned in the nick of time and chased the snake into a different room.

Anetta picked herself up and turned to leave, but when she did so, she heard a voice behind her.

Anetta turned around to see who it was. At the end of the hall stood a tall and creepy man.

His hair, which had once been black, was going prematurely white despite the fact that he was about the same age as Anetta.

His clothes, which had once been white, were now tarnished as if he had rolled in soot.

He wore his hair in a mullet and it was sticking up everywhere.

The man smelt badly, as if he hadn't bathed in a very long time.

"Who are you?" asked Anetta, trying not to seem afraid.

"I am Lord Doomlock, Prince of Darkness." Said the stranger.

"Don't you all say that?" Asked Anetta with a frown. She was clearly having a bad day, and it wasn't getting any better either. At this point, Anetta had completely lost her filter.

Doomlock just ignored Anetta's question.

"Well, my dear," He said.

"Now that you know who I am, please tell me who are you and what are you doing in my home?"

"I'm the daughter of the king, and I'm not your dear," said Anetta.

Doomlock let out a bought of mad laughter when Anetta said this, after which he uttered something so blasphemous that I don't care to soil my pin with its description.

"So, daughter of the King, what are you doing in my castle?"

"I suppose you're planning on cutting my head off with your father's sword?"

"Yes, I am," said Anetta in a sharp tone of voice.

"I am going to cut your head off with my father's sword. And when I do, I'll parade your head through every city street and village square from Merrick to Duchaine so that all the world may know that God is not to be mocked!"

Doomlock scrutinized Anetta for a moment, and when he didn't see a sword strapped to her hip, he let out another bout of mad laughter.

However, Anetta did indeed have her father's sword, but it was strapped to her back rather than her hip because it was just more comfortable for her to ride her horse that way.

The sword could not be seen by Doomlock, though, because she wore a heavy winter cloak which concealed her weapon from his sight. Doomlock just assumed that Anetta had come there unarmed because he couldn't see her weapon, and that was his first mistake.

Anetta's eyes narrowed when she suddenly noticed that Doomlock was slowly inching his way closer and closer to her, and the thing which he was leaning on was not a staff. Rather, it was a sword.

For you see, he had actually come to kill Anetta, and he was only trying to keep her talking so that he wouldn't have to run her down first.

He totally underestimated her, though, by assuming that she would simply come unarmed to his castle. Doomlock, however, had no idea who he was really talking to. The last time they met, Anetta was half-conscious and covered in her own blood because she had just received a brutal beating from Victor and Larson. If Doomlock had known who she really was, he certainly would have been at least a bit more cautious as he approached her.

"I see you have visited my aviary, my dear."

"Most of the birds were from my father's collection but I have added a few new birds of my own."

"Feel free to take as many birds as you like."

"Only you can't take the boy named Griffin."

"He has sold himself to me, and so now he's mine!"

When he said this, Doomlock stretched out his hand, and the red Falcon who had perched himself on Anetta's shoulder suddenly left her and went to perch on Doomlock's forearm.

"He's no longer yours because his ransom has been paid snapped Anetta angrily."

"OK, small one." Said Doomlock in a condescending tone of voice.

"But how can you prove it? What have you done for him anyway?"

Anetta's blood started boiling the moment Doomlock called her small one because it was commonly known that Brother John often called people little one when he babbled. But all of a sudden, she got the sense that she was no longer talking to Doomlock anymore, for neither his voice nor his eyes seemed his own at this point.

Anetta quickly took off her boots. As she did so, Doomlock pulled a silver chain out of his pocket and was about to fix it around Trestan's neck.

But just as soon as Anetta got her shoes off her feet, the chain in Doomlock's hand disappeared in a cloud of smoke.

When the chain disappeared, the Falcon flew back to Anetta and perched on her shoulder once again.

"I know someone who can help you," said Anetta, who was filled with pity for Doomlock.

The man was obviously sick, just like Trestan was when she first met him. Anetta desperately wanted to help the man in front of her, but Doomlock did not want help, though, and as soon as Anetta offered it to him, he began swinging his sword at her like a madman while lunging for her in a crazed fashion.

While they were talking Doomlock had managed to inch himself quite close to Anetta, and it wasn't long before he was close enough to be a threat with his weapon.

Anetta found it quite difficult to dodge the blows from his sword, but finally, Anetta swung back at Doomlock with her own weapon, and since she hit her mark perfectly, her blade took Doomlock's head clean off his shoulders.

The look of surprise which came to his face when Anetta drew her sword was still frozen there, when his head rolled across the floor. After taking a moment to clean the blood off her blade, she grabbed Doomlock's head just as she had promised and hobbled back in the direction from which she came.

But before she could even make it outside, she heard the snake coming up behind her.

She didn't dare look behind her. She just scrambled away from the snake with all her might despite her broken ankle and the horrible pain in her side.

When she finally came to a flight of steps that led outside, she scrambled up them, but when she got halfway to the top of them, she fell backward.

Anetta landed flat on her back on the floor. The giant serpent hovered over Anetta for a moment, and Alexander, Trestan, and Ella all took refuge under her cloak.

Anetta closed her eyes because she thought she was going to die, but just then, the eagle reappeared seemingly out of nowhere. No sooner did he land than he was transformed into a tall, strong-armed knight with broad shoulders.

He was completely dressed in shiny silver armor. He was wearing a closed helmet, so Anetta could not see his face.

When the eagle was transformed into a man the giant serpent was also transformed into a man as well.

"Step aside, Darius," hissed the knight in black armor. "She's mine, and you know it!"

"Ohh, you can have her over my dead body!" Said Darius as he drew a huge two-headed axe from his belt.

The black Knight drew a curved-bladed sword from its sheath, and the two men began to fight.

Anetta once knew a woman who bragged that she enjoyed it when men fought over her. As far as Anetta was concerned, though, it really wasn't as thrilling as some seemed to think, and it certainly wasn't her cup of tea, especially if both men had weapons and were swinging them right above her head.

The two men swung at each other frantically, and finally, after what seemed like an eternity to Anetta, Darius finally overcame his opponent and hit him in the throat with his ax.

When this happened, the black Knight just simply disappeared into a cloud of smoke that stank like sulfur.

As soon as the Knight in black vanished, the man named Darius took off his helmet to reveal the face of a fair and handsome youth.

The young man introduced himself to Anetta. "I am Darius, Your Majesty, and I am deeply indebted to you for what you have done for me. I have been stuck in the form of an eagle until someone brave enough would come and release me from my chains so that I could kill Lord Karthy and break the curse which was placed upon me by Lord Deathrogane. I've been stuck as a pooka for far too long, and none of my prayers could release me from my chains. Now that I am free, I am so happy that I could hug you, my lady."

"Watch it," said Anetta. "The last time a man stood too close to me without my permission, he suffered a swift end." As she said this, she held up Doomlock's severed head.

"Don't worry, my lady," said Darius with a little chuckle. "I have the greatest respect for your personal space."

"So if the curse was lifted, why are you still here?" Asked Anetta sharply.

"Why haven't you just moved on to the next World."

"Well," said Darius. "I wouldn't have normally even been able to take human form again, but because of the compassion you had on us, I was granted 3 days more in human form so that I could help you break the enchantment on your friends here."

"And we must make haste, for they don't have much time left." Now that they're out of their cages, they only have three days before they die."

"We must take them to the well in the center of the forest, tie them up in your cloak, and drop them in the well."

"That should break the curse."

"Well, come on," said Darius impatiently.

Anetta tried to stand, but she was unable to do so any longer, so Darius picked her up and carried her to the well so that she could break the enchantment.

They arrived at the well right before the sun rose on the third day, and Anetta was so weak at this point that she could hardly complete her task before collapsing near the well. And this was probably because she had lost so much blood on account of the wound that she sustained when Doomlock hit her in the chest with his sword.

As the first light of dawn on the third day filtered through the branches of the leafless trees of the forest, Darius disappeared into thin air. There was a sudden flash of light that came from the well when the curse was lifted, and shortly after this happened, Trestan, Alexander and Ella all woke near the well. They found Anetta's body not far from where they were. She was very cold and very close to death. They tried to revive her by warming her up. When they took her armor off in an effort to worm her, they found a letter she had written to her mother.

Anetta had planned on delivering it herself. However, she died on a Friday at the very same moment that Gregor breathed his last.

It really was as though the two were twin souls, and it seemed as though they had accomplished their last quest together despite the fact that they were so far away from each other.

On the day that Anetta killed Doomlock, Karegan was sitting at daily mass and the great cathedral in the capital city of Duchene. He suddenly felt a terrible pain in his side. It was as if he was being stabbed by an invisible hand. And the blade was splitting him clean down one side. The king was in so much pain that he could hardly move, and Malkovich was forced to carry him out to his coach. When he was finally brought back to his own bed chambers, he was laid in his bed, and his mother called the physician.

The King's physician, however, did not find anything wrong with Karegan. After three days, at exactly 3 o'clock in the afternoon, the stabbing pain in Karegan's side suddenly vanished. You would think that he would be greatly relieved; however, he most certainly was not. In fact, Karegan was filled with alarm when the pain vanished.

As he got dressed, he headed towards Gregor's room. Anetta kept popping into his head as he walked. "What have I done? " Thought Karegan as he walked quickly in the direction of Gregor's bed chambers. "Have I sent my sister to her grave?"

"Will I ever see her again?"

Karegan's thoughts were troubling, to say the least, and although he tried desperately just to put it out of his head, he most certainly could not.

By the time Karegan made it to Gregor's bed chambers, the captain of the palace guards had already died.

Karegan sank to his knees at the foot of Gregor's bed and wept bitterly over the death of his friend. Karegan also wept for his sister for he greatly feared that he would never see her again either.

When Karegan finally calmed down, he started looking around Gregor's room and it was rather a plain one. It had a bed and a writing desk, and the only other things that Gregor kept in the room were things that Anetta had given him when she was a child.

On Gregor's writing desk was every flower that Anetta had ever picked him as a girl. They were all wilted, of course. Just above the little writing desk, which Gregor used as a shrine, hung a picture of the Madonna and Child, which Anetta had drawn for him. The picture was terribly disproportionate. However, Gregor thought it was beautiful, and he would often say his rosary in front of that picture.

When several man servants entered the room to take Gregor's body away, Karegan told them to leave the room exactly as it was because he was terribly afraid that all he had left of his sister was contained in that room.

Gregor's death was a terrible one, and he suffered a great deal when he was dying.

The stroke he had suffered paralyzed him. And because he could no longer move, he developed bed sores. After this, things went from bad to worse. First, he got gangrene, then blood poisoning, which finally killed him. Karegan knelt by Gregor's little shrine, and as he did so, he found himself marveling over Gregor's courage.

The man had utterly refused to take anything for the pain when they operated on his leg.

The King's physician simply claimed that Gregor had gotten brain damage when he had his stroke, and he couldn't feel the pain. Karegan knew better than to believe that because he was there when Gregor agreed to become a victim soul.

Just as many mourners attended Gregor's funeral as they did when King Ruben the Second died, and the great cathedral was terribly inadequate for the number of people who showed up to mourn the passing of the palace guard.

Lord Gregor was buried with great honor. After the funeral, Karegan took some time to sit by himself in Gregor's room. As he sat there, he wondered if Anetta really was dead. Still, he hoped in divine Providence.

While Anetta did not manage to end the reign of darkness that had descended upon the land, she did manage to stifle its growing power. This is because darkness will always exist in this world as long as rebellion against the Divine Master does. Doomlock's severed head was found by an ambitious man, and he may have been even more wicked than Doomlock was. This man took over Doomlock's coven.

There was no minstrel to sing about their heroism. No poet to write about Gregors and Anetta's great deed, but words often lie. However, kindness never does, and it kind person is worth their weight in gold. They also bring a great deal of light to this dark and dreary world because they reflect so perfectly the light of their Divine Master.

My name is Brother Trestan of God, and I relate this story to you out of obedience to my superior so that you may know the great value of compassion and purity of heart. If you're so lucky to have a mother, may you kiss her often on the cheek and tell her you love her, whether or not you agree with her. And no matter what you do, never, never, ever play with snakes! But if my tail is late in reaching you and you've already chosen that dark and cruel master, either by playing with snakes or in any other way, May you turn to the Divine and Almighty Master of all and throw yourself upon His loving mercy. Although my tail has many embellishments to make it more interesting. It still rings true, and I hope that you find it inspirational, whether you are wild, brave, or foolish.

To be continued. . .

Moucavich

Prince of Ricknorerack and
Karegan's bodyguard

Lord Dairius

Shape Shifter, Assassin

Lord Lackmore

Witch Assassin, Palace Guard,
Ella's half brother

Lord Karthy

Shape Shifter, Assassin

Lady Ella
Victom Soul, Visionary,
Lackmore's Half Sister

Anetta
Victim Soul, Warrior Princess,
Karagan's Twin Sister

Drago
Palace Guard, Assassin

King Deathrogane
Powerful Wizard. Father to
Doomlock and Darius

Michellie
Palace Guard/Penitent

Rin
Garic's Son, Mystic & Spy

Brother Malcolm
Father guest master at the
Santa Dalo Rosa

Father Ivan
Pious old Abbott at the
Santa Dalo Rosa

Brother Lucas
Brother porter at the
Santa Dalo Rosa

Brother John
Prince, Priest & Visionary

Garic
Mystic, Deacon, Witch Hunter

Karegan
High Prince of Duchaine,
Mystic, Anetta's Twin Brother